Cape Perdido

Also by Marcia Muller
in Large Print:

Leave a Message for Willie
Point Deception
A Walk Through the Fire
While Other People Sleep
Wolf in the Shadows
Cyanide Wells
The Dangerous Hour
Dead Midnight

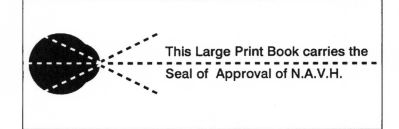

This Large Print Book carries the
Seal of Approval of N.A.V.H.

Cape Perdido

MARCIA MULLER

Thorndike Press • Waterville, Maine

Published in 2005 by arrangement with
Warner Books, Inc.

Thorndike Press® Large Print Americana.

The tree indicium is a trademark of Thorndike Press.

The text of this Large Print edition is unabridged.
Other aspects of the book may vary from the original edition.

Set in 16 pt. Plantin.

Printed in the United States on permanent paper.

Library of Congress Cataloging-in-Publication Data

Muller, Marcia.
    Cape Perdido / by Marcia Muller.
       p. cm. — (Thorndike Press large print Americana)
    ISBN 0-7862-7931-1 (lg. print : hc : alk. paper)
    1. Community life — Fiction.   2. Corporations —
Fiction.   3. California — Fiction.   4. Large type books.
I. Title.   II. Thorndike Press large print Americana series.
PS3563.U397C37 2005b

                   2005014751

For the high-stakes gamblers:
Bette and Jim Lamb
Peggy and Charlie Lucke
Who's light?

As the Founder/CEO of NAVH, the only national health agency solely devoted to those who, although not totally blind, have an eye disease which could lead to serious visual impairment, I am pleased to recognize Thorndike Press★ as one of the leading publishers in the large print field.

Founded in 1954 in San Francisco to prepare large print textbooks for partially seeing children, NAVH became the pioneer and standard setting agency in the preparation of large type.

Today, those publishers who meet our standards carry the prestigious "Seal of Approval" indicating high quality large print. We are delighted that Thorndike Press is one of the publishers whose titles meet these standards. We are also pleased to recognize the significant contribution Thorndike Press is making in this important and growing field.

Lorraine H. Marchi, L.H.D.
Founder/CEO
NAVH

★ Thorndike Press encompasses the following imprints: Thorndike, Wheeler, Walker and Large Print Press.

Many thanks to the following individuals, who aided and abetted me:

Sam Parsons, EMT, South Coast VFD, Medic 120 — and Renaissance Man

Melissa Ward, tireless researcher

Kristen Weber, who stepped in at a very bad time and is doing a great job

And Bill, who again has survived the transitions from Marcia Jekyll to Marcia Hyde, and vice versa

And thanks also to the Friends of the Gualala River, who fought to preserve our corner of paradise

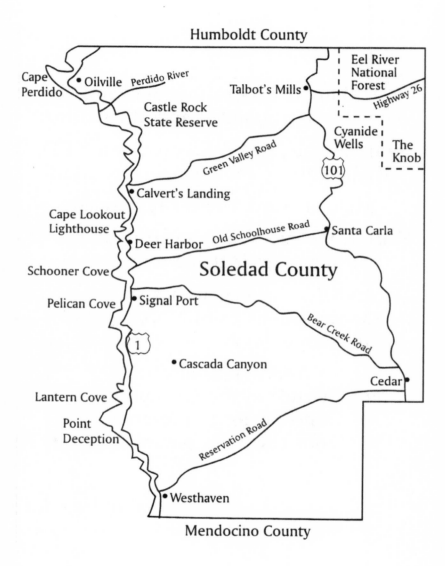

The River

From its source deep in the wilderness on Soledad Ridge, the clear, cold water of the Perdido River begins its journey to the sea. Twenty-seven miles of mostly navigable water held in the California Public Trust because it is deemed too valuable for individual ownership.

A protected place — for now.

Imagine yourself standing near the spring where the river rushes from the earth. It flows rapidly, leaping and bounding over boulders that churn it to whitewater. Ancient redwoods crowd in upon its rocky banks, shafts of sunlight penetrating their dense foliage. The cry of a hawk splits the silence, and you look up in time to see it soar against the blue sky.

You follow the river miles downstream, to where it widens and moves under eucalyptus, tanbark oak, and pine. Its banks are reed choked, a nesting place for waterfowl. A great blue heron cranes its long neck, and an osprey rises up, its wings beating the air. Sun dapples the flanks of the coho salmon and steelhead trout that have swum upstream to spawn, and you spot the sleek brown flash of a river otter as it plays in the current. You sniff air laden with pine resin and the peculiar, mentholated odor of eucalyptus.

This is a place out of time — for now.

West, where the Perdido eases off to sea level, it moves lazily around sandbars and between white sand beaches, carrying with it kayakers, swimmers, and dogs splashing after Frisbees their owners have tossed. Many of these people are locals, but most are tourists, drawn here by the river's recreational activities. Tourists, who are the lifeblood of Cape Perdido, the seaside town to the north. You watch them and think it is wonderful that all this has been preserved in its natural state for everyone's enjoyment.

Preserved — for now.

Friday, February 20

Jessie Domingo

"Three-three-Sierra, turning final."

Jessie gripped the seat with both hands and stared at the back of the charter pilot's head, hoping he was as calm and capable as he sounded. Through the tiny plane's window she saw nothing but pine trees stretching toward the placid gray sea.

Where the hell was the runway?

"Make sure your seat belts're fastened tight, folks. We'll be on the ground in a couple of minutes."

Thank God!

She yanked on the end of the belt so hard that it all but forced the air from her lungs, then glanced at her traveling companion, Fitch Collier, for reassurance. Wouldn't you know it? The lawyer was sprawled out in his seat, sound asleep.

What an asshole!

First he'd upgraded to business class on their flight from New York, leaving her with her knees pressed against her nose in coach. Then he'd proceeded to wander back and forth between their seats the whole time, bringing her documents he'd finished reading, and annoying the other two passengers in the cramped row by leaning across them to issue comments and instructions. And now he was comatose, just as the pilot of the little four-seater got set to plunge them into a thick forest in the wilds of northern California!

Where the hell *is that runway?*

The tops of the trees came level with the window. Jessie felt as if she were being sucked down a steep green chute. She closed her eyes, her ears popped, and then the plane thumped onto the ground so hard that pain shot up her spine. She tried to remember if her health plan paid for chiropractic treatment.

When the pain cleared and she opened her eyes, the plane was turning toward a low brown prefab terminal where two figures stood in a patch of pale winter sunlight. The welcoming committee from the Friends of the Perdido River. An ancient, mud-splattered white van was the only vehicle in sight. If this was to be their ground transportation, Jessie hoped it had good suspension.

Beside her, Fitch stretched and yawned — a honking sound that reminded her of a recent *National Geographic* special on Canadian geese. She glared at him before she felt around at her feet for her briefcase. Predictably, he didn't notice.

She'd met Fitch Collier, as prearranged by her employer, in the boarding area at Kennedy a long ten hours before. Already she was beginning to loathe him. Besides the upgrading and the kibitzing from the aisle, he'd spent their entire layover in San Francisco on his cellular, talking to more people than Jessie even knew about a variety of subjects designed to impress anyone within the greater Bay Area. From these conversations Jessie had learned, among other things, that Fitch expected to make a small fortune on the upcoming IPO of SoftTech, that the Benz was being repainted, that he was still searching for a good deal on a time-share on St. Bart's, that "the babe" couldn't get enough of him.

In short, Fitch was an ostentatious, inconsiderate jerk — all the more so because he made her feel mean-spirited for disliking him so much after so short an acquaintance.

When she'd drawn this assignment, Jessie had been excited — what community liaison specialist at Environmental Consultants Clearinghouse wouldn't have been? An opportunity to work with Fitch, one of the best water rights attorneys in the country. A trip to a remote part of the northern California coast. A complex and potentially precedent-setting case that, should they win it, would earn them front-page coverage in newspapers across the country.

Jessie Domingo, in the *New York Times*!

Jessie Domingo, on *Sixty Minutes*!

Jessie Domingo, stuck at the end of nowhere with an egomaniacal, dictatorial lawyer who clearly considered her a mere flunky. And who, should they succeed, would end up taking all the credit for their joint efforts.

Reality strikes. Jessie strikes out — again.

The pilot shut down the plane, and Jessie peered out at the pair by the terminal. The stocky woman in the voluminous multicolored skirt and cape would be Bernina Tobin, and the lanky denim-clad man with the cloud of silver-gray curls, Joseph Openshaw. From both her reading of the foundation's research files and her phone conversations with Bernina, Jessie knew that she was a Maine transplant and had led the Friends of the Perdido River in their yearlong battle against a water grab by Aqueduct Systems, Inc., a North

Carolina corporation. Openshaw had been one of Jessie's heroes ever since she became interested in ecology. A nationally known environmental activist and author and a native of the Cape Perdido area, he'd returned from the state capital early in the fight to lend his support and had done much to turn public opinion against the waterbaggers, as the locals called them.

Jessie and Fitch had been sent by ECC to Cape Perdido in order to familiarize themselves firsthand with the situation; they would consult with local experts in hydrology and ecosystems, as well as with the leaders of the protests and other residents of the area. Next week they would journey to Sacramento, where Fitch would argue their case before the state water resources control board. If all went well, they would score a major coup for pro-environmental groups; if not, the board would rule to allow a pumping station to be built upstream on the Perdido, and pipe laid across a defunct lumber company's mill site, where the river's waters would be sucked into massive rubberized bags moored offshore, to be towed south and sold to drought-starved southern California municipalities such as San Diego.

Leaving the community with no recompense for its loss.

Leaving the ecology of the Perdido permanently damaged, and a visual blight on what was now a pristine and beautiful coastline.

Leaving the door open for violence in a place where the citizens had long embraced the tradition of taking the law into their own hands when the law didn't suit them.

The challenge was clear. Jessie stepped down from the plane, prepared to embrace it.

Joseph Openshaw

"Here come the New Yorkers."

Joseph ignored Bernina Tobin's comment and folded his arms across his chest, squinting at the luggage-laden pair moving toward them. What in God's name did they have in those suitcases?

The woman was very attractive, tall and slender with straight, light brown hair that swirled about her shoulders in the strong breeze. The man was also tall, and very thin, with silver-rimmed glasses and blond hair that was styled in casual disarray. They were dressed in what city dwellers always assumed was proper attire for the wilderness: pressed jeans, stylish sweaters, brand-new down jackets, designer walking shoes. Within a week, the jeans would be rumpled, the sweaters in need of dry cleaning, the jackets mud-stained, and the shoes replaced by sturdy boots from Perdido Feed and Surplus.

Thanks for coming all this way, strangers. And welcome to a world you can't begin to understand. No offense, but I doubt there's

19

anything you can do for us.

Joseph unfolded his arms and, nudging Bernina forward, went to greet the visitors.

"You must be Ms. Tobin," the young woman said, extending her hand to Bernina. The heavy bag she had slung over her left shoulder slipped free and landed in the crook of her elbow. Momentarily she was thrown off balance and bumped against her traveling companion, who frowned in annoyance.

"Call me Bernina," Tobin told her. "You're Jessie, of course, and you're Fitch." She nodded at the man. "And this is Joseph."

Joseph relieved Jessie Domingo of the uncooperative bag and returned Fitch Collier's stiff nod with a smile.

"This all your stuff?" Bernina asked.

"Pilot's unloading the rest." Collier gestured at the plane.

Joseph glanced over there, saw Al Raymond, the regular on the charter flights from San Francisco to Soledad County, dragging two more bags from the luggage compartment. Jesus, they really didn't travel light! Each had gotten off the plane with a briefcase and a large duffel, and Collier carried a hanging bag. Maybe it contained his golfing clothes — or his formal attire?

Joseph went to help Al load the luggage into the back of his van while Bernina got the delegation from ECC settled inside.

When the offer of assistance in the Friends of the Perdido's opposition to the waterbaggers had come from Environmental Consultants Clearinghouse's executive director, Joseph had felt uneasy. Not that ECC didn't have an excellent track record. A nonprofit foundation funded by grants from corporations and wealthy philanthropists, it employed a full-time administrative staff and called upon a large panel of attorneys and other professionals specializing in a wide spectrum of environmental issues. When the foundation took on a cause, it would pair the various experts, such as Fitch Collier, with an on-staff community liaison specialist — in this case, Jessie Domingo — and send them into the field to gather information. This method created a picture of the situation that encompassed the legal, technical, and sociological issues. More often than not, ECC was able to work out environmentally favorable solutions through the appropriate legal channels.

Now, viewing the pair that had been sent west, Joseph's unease returned. In spite of her confident manner, the woman couldn't be much more than twenty-five, and the man, while closer to his own age, reminded him of the fresh-faced fraternity boys he'd known at UC Berkeley who laughed and played their way through the world, oblivious to the fact that it was swiftly going to hell. Neither of these people seemed capable of dealing with the volatile situation that was shaping up at Cape Perdido.

But it was Eldon Whitesides, ECC's director, who really raised the level of Joseph's discomfort. He and Whitesides had come up together in the environmental wars of the eighties at Berkeley but had long since followed divergent paths. Whitesides's route led him into the rarefied realm of important political connections and substantial philanthropic backing, while Joseph's led to the grassroots, poorly financed ghetto. While Whitesides made compromises and hammered out agreements in well-appointed parlors and boardrooms, Joseph held to a hard line in storefronts and on the streets. Not once in the year that the Friends of the Perdido had opposed the North Carolina water-exporting firm's proposed project had Eldon Whitesides taken notice of the battle raging in Soledad County — a battle whose outcome might very well determine the way water rights were handled throughout the state, and perhaps the country, for decades to come.

So why, when the hearings before the state water resources control board were so near, had Whitesides surfaced with his offer to help?

Joseph slammed the van's back doors, mock-saluted Al, and went around to the driver's side. Bernina sat half turned in the passenger's seat, chattering at the new-comers in her Down East accent. Something flattering about the Shorebird Motel and the Blue Moon Cafe, obviously trying to paint an appealing picture of what to outsiders would seem a pretty drab coastal outpost on a winter day. He started the van, only half listening, and drove down the access road of the small airport. At least Tobin wasn't getting dogmatic on them just yet.

He didn't dislike Bernina, but an uneasy and sometimes prickly philosophical truce existed between them. She embraced the principles of feminist ecology — which Joseph, in a self-admittedly paranoid and simplistic fashion, interpreted as the view that everything wrong with the natural world was the direct result of men's piggish behavior toward it. Although he didn't like to think in terms of labels, if he had to characterize himself according to the currently accepted guidelines, Joseph would say he was a social ecologist. Which, once the fancy rhetoric was stripped away, meant a practical person who believed there were ways for humans and nature to coexist in health and harmony. Throughout the six months since his return to Cape Perdido, Bernina — who was also his landlady — had spiritedly lectured him about the wrongness of his beliefs, insisting that if he'd only admit that a patriarchical society had fucked up the earth, he'd be on his way to enlightenment.

To Joseph, she sounded like the missionaries who used to come around to convert the coastal Pomos, a tribe with whom he had blood ties: cast off your heathen religion, accept our teachings, repent your sins, and the kingdom of heaven is yours.

From the corner of his eye he saw Bernina glance at him, a frown that said she thought he was being inhospitable knitting her thick eyebrows. "Oilville coming up," he said, too heartily.

Jessie Domingo asked, "Why's it called that? I don't recall from my reading."

Bernina said, "It's the site of one of the first oil fields in California. Most people think all the state's oil wells are in southern

California, but there was a short-lived boom here in the mid-eighteen-sixties. After the wells dried up, so did the town. Now that's what's left." She motioned at the lone gas station and convenience store, the scattering of small frame houses that nestled in a clearing upon which the thick forest was slowly encroaching.

The lawyer, Fitch Collier, hadn't spoken or moved since they left the airport. With some concern, Joseph glanced into the rearview mirror. No, not dead, just sleeping.

Bernina went on. "Cape Perdido is a different story. The lumber mill, first called Breyer's, and then McNear's, was built there in eighteen-sixty-three. The Cape became a doghole port, where schooners would take on lumber for transport south to San Francisco. Generation after generation worked that mill, but the decline in the lumbering industry forced its owner to shut it down five years ago, and now — well, you know from the press coverage about Timothy McNear offering to let Aqueduct Systems lay the pipe for their operation across the site. Anyway, the Cape's managed to hang on economically because of tourism and recreational opportunities. And people like me, who enjoy the small-town atmosphere and natural beauty, are still moving there — although there's no telling what'll happen if those waterbaggers succeed in raping our river. And 'rape' is the right word for it. I can draw a lot of parallels between a violent sex crime and what that man, Gregory Erickson, wants to do here."

Please don't start, Joseph thought. Not now. Let these tired people get settled in before you try to indoctrinate them.

To turn the conversation in another direction, he said, "Bernina's a real authority on our little piece of the earth, even though she only came out from Maine three years ago."

Immediately he regretted the way it sounded. Bernina's eyes narrowed and she glared at him. "I suppose *you're* an authority, even though you abandoned this 'little piece of the earth' twenty years ago?"

He was not going to argue with her in front of strangers. "Oh, look, folks!" he exclaimed, pointing skyward. "There's a golden eagle!"

As they craned their necks to spot the nonexistent bird, he accelerated toward the turnoff for Cape Perdido.

Steph Pace

Steph let the fishnet curtain fall against the front window of the Blue Moon. Anxiety tickled at the base of her spine like restless fingers.

Get a grip, woman!

Joseph and Bernina were checking the New Yorkers into the Shorebird Motel, across Highway 1. Once finished there, he would come over for his afternoon cup of coffee, and she didn't want him to see her in this state. He'd notice that something was wrong — he noticed everything — and he'd ask what had happened. And then she'd have to lie — something she didn't do very well to him — or else explain, which would open up the very can of worms that last week he'd told her to close and keep closed.

If only Timothy McNear hadn't chosen this morning to try out the Blue Moon's breakfast special for the first time in the eleven years Steph had owned the café. He remembered her, though, and his dark eyes had bored into hers from under shaggy

27

gray brows, their intensity belying his mild "Good morning, Miss Stephanie." It was as if he could see into her mind and read the secrets hidden there, of which there were quite a few. One in particular she suspected he knew, and why he'd chosen to keep it to himself for two decades was a question whose answer she didn't care to probe.

What amazed her was that Timothy McNear dared to show his face in the village at all these days. Five years ago, when he'd shut down his family's lumber mill, the public's reaction had been angry, and McNear had stayed in his big house on the ridge for many months, until the anger gradually smoldered to resentment and then dissipated entirely. But now, when he'd committed the ultimate traitorous act of offering access across the mill site to those waterbaggers . . . Well, rage was too mild a term for the collective emotion directed at him.

Stupid, Steph thought, for McNear to venture forth in a place where, to many of the residents, guns were a natural appendage to be exercised whenever the mood struck them.

Stupid. Or arrogant. Or something else entirely.

From the kitchen behind her, Steph heard the sounds of chopping as the cook prepared the last of the ingredients for that night's fish chowder. An hour to go till the waitresses arrived; an hour more till the dinner service began. She could go home for the interim and avoid Joseph, who would be just as glad to chat up the cook while having his coffee. A nap or a bath might temporarily ease her anxiety.

She raised the curtain again and looked out at the Shorebird. Standard motel: two stories of cinder block, its white paint weathered by the strong winds off the Pacific. A huge rusted anchor and chain lay in a thick patch of ice plant in front of the office; a rotting fishing dory in a similar patch in front of the near wing of units. Tourists traveling Highway 1 either found the place quaint and didn't mind the plain accommodations, or went inland to Highway 101 or south to the better-appointed and AAA-recommended motels at Calvert's Landing. Most days, the Shorebird's vacancy sign was lit twenty-four hours, but today it had been turned off. The reason being visitors coming to town for tomorrow afternoon's viewing of the type of water bag Aqueduct Systems planned to use to haul the river water, and the open forum where the company's CEO would answer questions and present his case. A van from the county's lone television station already stood before one of the motel rooms.

Steph automatically glanced at the far wing, where Gregory Erickson, president of the North Carolina firm, and his staff were staying, then back at Joseph's van near the opposite end of the building. At least the desk clerk had thought to place the New Yorkers as far away from the Aqueduct people as possible. Steph would caution her waitresses to do the same, should both parties show up at the same time for dinner. When local rivalries raised their ugly little heads, a delicate balancing act was required of Cape Perdido's only real restaurant, but the simultaneous presence of the New Yorkers and the North Carolinians had the potential to spawn something far more serious than a small-town pissing contest.

That particular combination was the stuff that small-town nightmares were made of.

Timothy McNear

Timothy eased into his big leather chair, set his glass of single-malt Scotch on the side table, and pulled the thick Hudson's Bay blanket over his lap. Once settled comfortably — as much as a man of seventy-four who suffers from arthritis can hope — he trained his eyes on the line where sea met sky. It was not a pronounced line this evening, the day having been dull and overcast, but as always, it called out to him.

For the past thirty-some years, it had been Timothy's custom to climb the ladder to the loft above the kitchen of his rambling redwood house at precisely seven minutes before sunset. In the early days, the climb had been easy, and he'd had ample time to pour his Scotch and get settled before the show — or, as today, the lack thereof — began. Then, about ten years ago, he'd noticed a shortness of breath and the need of a few moments to regain equilibrium before the pouring ceremony; now sharp pains in his legs and back slowed his climbing, and he often put off handling the crystal carafe until he was seated, the blanket securely tucked around him against the gathering chill.

Aging is a bitch, but I can still make it up here and get settled in seven minutes. The day I can't is when I pack it in. There are some things a man must not surrender to.

The horizon was blurring now, gray melding into gray — a color appropriate to Timothy's thoughts. Tomorrow he must dress in his best suit and go down to the point where McNear's had once milled some of the finest lumber and railroad ties in northern California. Smile agreeably as the Aqueduct Systems delegation tried to persuade the townspeople that their plans would not put a blight on the coastline. Turn a brave face to the people he'd betrayed not once but twice.

They don't even hate me. They hold me in contempt.

He'd seen it on the faces of Miss Stephanie's customers when he'd entered her restaurant that morning. Seen it on the face of the waitress — one of the Puska twins; he couldn't tell which. Most of the diners had paid up and left in a hurry. He'd spoiled their breakfasts, probably their lunches and dinners, too.

So why had he gone there?

Timothy took a sip of Scotch, contemplated the question as he watched the horizon disappearing.

Maybe he'd just been curious: test the waters, see what was in store for him the next afternoon. Maybe he'd been in a masochistic mood: let them have at him beforehand. Or maybe he'd wanted to see if a different sort of contempt for him still lived in Miss Stephanie's eyes, a contempt only matched by that he felt for himself.

Well, if the latter was his true reason, he'd gotten what he wanted — and then some more. There had been fear in Stephanie Pace's eyes, too. Why should she fear him at this late date? He was an old man, and he'd kept his silence.

Miss Stephanie. Former live-in nanny to his grandsons. His only son, Robert, had brought the boys to live with Timothy twenty years ago, after their mother died of breast cancer, thinking a change of scene from the Bay Area would do them good. Robert continued working at his job as a graphic designer in San Francisco during the week, commuting on the weekends. Timothy, never good with children, struggled to be a surrogate parent to the troubled children, but it quickly became apparent he needed more help than his housekeeper could provide. So Miss Stephanie came to live in the big house on the ridge. And then began the series of events that had led to Timothy's present predicament.

All of that done and gone, years back. It shouldn't matter now — to her, to me, or anyone else. Why can't I face it and put things right?

Timothy sipped Scotch and contemplated yet another difficult question as he watched the horizon disappear.

Jessie Domingo

In the fading light of the afternoon, Jessie sat on the lumpy bed in the little motel room, throwing herself a pity party.

Party? Try gala!

It was the time of day that, in winter, always depressed her. Not only that, but the room smelled strongly of disinfectant, everything felt damp, the water tap dripped, and the yellowed shades on the lamps made the furnishings look so dingy that she'd turned the lights off. Through the wall she could hear Fitch, who had been horrified to find that his cellular provider had no sites on this side of the coastal ridge, on his room's phone to one of his seemingly endless supply of friends. Jessie had tried to call Erin Sullivan, her roommate in New York, but had gotten only their machine. The thought of her announcement of her safe arrival echoing in the pretty, empty apartment, combined with the relative squalor of her present surroundings, had nearly reduced her to tears.

Come on, Jess, the place isn't so bad, and

besides, this is an adventure.

Some adventure.

She had, of course, known that Soledad County was one of the smallest and poorest in California. Bordered on the north by Humboldt County and on the south by Mendocino, it stretched eastward beyond the boundaries of the Eel River National Forest and into the foothills of the Sierra Nevada. Historically, lumbering and fishing had been the mainstays of its economy, but with the decline of both those industries, the handful of small towns along the coast and inland on the Highway 101 corridor had turned to tourism for their sustenance. The prevalence of low-paying service-industry jobs kept the per-capita income and standard of living low. One report prepared for Jessie and Fitch by the foundation's research staff had made a tongue-in-cheek reference to deeply entrenched marijuana growers and manufacturers of other controlled substances as the county's aristocrats.

And now this town . . .

From the airstrip near the tiny settlement of Oilville, Joseph Openshaw had driven them along a winding road through a gap in the low, pine-forested hills and turned south onto Highway 1. The two-lane pavement ran along the top of a high bluff for some three miles before a cluster of buildings appeared in the distance. Huge rock formations, white with bird droppings, rose offshore, the waves smashing against them and spewing foam into the air.

The town itself was nothing more than a wide spot on the highway. Many of the establishments — a post office, feed-and-surplus, general store, bank, insurance agency, and real estate office — were of wood, with false fronts, like a set for a Western movie. The motel was a pair of undistinguished cinder-block ells; across the street on the ocean side stood a bar and restaurant of weatherbeaten brown shingles. Private residences of all types lined unpaved side streets or were strewn about on the slope of the hill without any seeming plan. Everything looked shabby and unkempt. Maybe in better weather the town was pretty, but, my God, what did people *do* here? How could they possibly stand it? It was so far from everything, and so shabby, so . . . downscale.

As her aunt on the Puerto Rican side of her family — her father's — was fond of reminding her, Jessie was a bit of a princess when it came to the thread count of her sheets. Meaning Mom and Dad had spoiled their youngest child with creature comforts. Jessie appreciated the material gifts bestowed upon her and knew her life had been blessed in ways that many other people's hadn't, but she valued far more her parents' other contributions: a solid work ethic, the encouragement to become her own person, the attitude that if she applied herself she could do whatever she wished.

A person who defines herself that way should not sit in the dark feeling sorry for herself. Right?

Jessie turned on the bedside lamp and went to get her briefcase so she could set up her laptop and once again go over her files and her notes on her conversations with Bernina Tobin. There was no data port in the room, but she jerry-rigged the machine into the phone, checked her e-mail — none of any importance — and set up a makeshift office on the small table.

As she read the files and considered what she might accomplish here, all traces of Jessie's homesickness vanished. The shabby motel room no longer depressed her, and she found herself looking forward to this evening's dinner meeting with members of the Friends. This was the kind

of fight she'd been dreaming of for years —
a chance to dig in her heels and make a
difference. A chance to finally prove she
could succeed at something on her own.

And maybe this time, I just might hit a home run.

Joseph Openshaw

Joseph looked down the long table that the waitress at the Blue Moon had assembled for their party, and surveyed those seated around it. Bernina. The New Yorkers. Various Friends of the Perdido. Curtis Hope.

Curtis Hope: ecologist, member of the tribal council of the local Pomos, friend of Joseph's youth, now semi-estranged. That was what a certain type of shared experience could do to early friendships, and between them, he and Curt had far too much baggage.

Bernina was in her element as she recounted for their guests the saga of the fight for the Perdido. Later, when they adjourned to her house for a general meeting, she would energize everyone as she outlined both ECC's purpose in coming to Cape Perdido and the Friends' plans for a protest at the public forum the following afternoon. The board members who had been invited to this dinner looked pumped up already; they'd spent long months passing out information on the water grab,

40

updating the Friends' Web site, contacting experts who might be willing to testify at the water board hearing, gathering signatures on petitions, and helping local property owners fill out protest forms for the state water resources control board. Mostly middle-aged or older, and veterans of decades-past movements, they were tired of those mundane but necessary activities, eager for action.

Jessie Domingo seemed to have caught their excitement and was listening attentively to Bernina. Fitch Collier, on the other hand, seemed disengaged; his gaze skipped restlessly around the room, surveying with some scorn the Blue Moon's nautical decor. Now and then his hand reached for his jacket pocket, then abruptly stopped. The man had nearly thrown a tantrum when he realized that his cellular phone service didn't have sites in the area, and he seemed incapable of untethering himself from the device.

Curtis must have noted the focus of Joseph's attention, because he raised his beer bottle in a mock toast, a cynical smile on his dark, sharp-planed face. His old friend, Joseph knew, was not impressed by the attorney's urbanity — would not be impressed were he sitting beside him in one of New York's finest restaurants. Curtis had concerns other than the worldly, and while Joseph could surmise some of them, of others he hadn't a clue.

Joseph turned his attention to his steak, glancing up now and then and half listening to the conversation around the table.

"That river is one of the treasures of northern California," Bernina was saying. "And it's the lifeblood of this town, too. Without the income from the campers and kayakers and sportsmen, Cape Perdido would dry up and blow away."

She paused, then said to Jessie and Fitch, "I know the town mustn't seem like much to you. You're seeing it on a dreary winter day. And, of course, it's about as different from New York as anything can get. But I'll tell you, when I came here on vacation from Maine, on a beautiful fall day, I fell in love with the area. So I went home, packed up, and moved."

Lee Longways, a tall, lanky rancher and longtime board member, added, "A lot of us have been here for generations. Both in the town and up on the ridge. The Cape's not just our home; it's a way of life. We have an affinity for the land and the sea. When we realized that commercial water harvesters could just come in and take what we've always considered ours, without putting back a dime into the community, well . . ." He shook his head, his weathered face creasing in a frown.

Jessie Domingo leaned forward. "That was in the spring, when you first became aware of the threat?"

"May, it was," Longways said. "Aqueduct Systems filed applications with the state water resources control board in January, requesting permission to siphon off eighty-six hundred acre-feet of water annually. That's a lot — yearly rainfall can amount to as little as thirty inches or as much as seventy-five, and if there were several drought years, the Perdido would be left with hardly any water at all. Anyway, it wasn't until May that Jane here caught wind of the applications and broke the story in the Calvert's Landing *Weekly Gazette*."

Jane White, a tall blonde reporter, laughed. "That's me — ever quick on the uptake. Actually, I'd heard rumors about the applications a couple of months before and alerted my editor, but at first we laughed them off. The idea of somebody taking our water for free and towing it to southern California in giant rubber bags . . . Well, it was too preposterous. But then,

43

when I began studying the regulations for California's public trust lands, I realized how serious the situation was. Lands in the public trust are defined as types of property of such high public value that private ownership should be limited, and they fall under control of the state. The water board has the right to grant Aqueduct Systems permission to siphon off water from the Perdido — a dangerous precedent for use of all California's navigable waterways."

"And," Bernina said, "there's good reason to fear that the board might rule in favor of the waterbaggers: their project would benefit southern California, which is the more politically powerful portion of the state."

Lee Longways's wife, Jenna, a strongly built white-haired woman who had been one of Joseph's grade-school teachers, nodded. "That's right. But political clout aside, the Friends have put up a good fight. We'd always been this little group of do-gooders. We'd go up and down the river dragging old tires and other junk out of the water, rally volunteers each spring to clean up dead trees and debris washed down by the winter storms, kept the beaches tidy in the summer when they're heavily used. We didn't know squat about mounting a campaign to influence the state to act in our best interests — but we learned fast."

"You bet we did," Bernina said. "Over the summer and fall, the Friends persuaded the Soledad County Board of Supervisors to pass a resolution protesting the water grab. We organized community meetings to raise public awareness of the danger to the environment, bringing in ecologists, hydrologists, and water rights attorneys — all of whom expressed negative opinions about Aqueduct Systems' project. Because Aqueduct's applications to the state were as yet incomplete, they declined to send representatives to any of our meetings."

Joseph realized that Jessie Domingo was looking at him, her eyebrows raised questioningly. Before he'd taken leave of her at the motel, she'd confided that he was one of her heroes, that she had read both books he'd authored, and had followed his career since college. She must be dismayed, he thought, to find her cultural icon more interested in a hunk of bloody meat than the spirited conversation, so he set down his fork and said, "The more people found out about what Aqueduct wanted to do, the more they got involved. Our local assemblyman contacted me in Sacramento, where I was living at the time, and asked me to help, so I moved back here in September."

"And really whipped us into shape," Lee Longways said.

"No, you whipped *yourselves* into shape." To Jessie Domingo, Joseph added, "They sent representatives to water board meetings to see how they operate. Gathered signatures on petitions. Showed property owners how to fill out forms protesting the grab. Then they reached out to other communities up and down the coast that might be vulnerable to this sort of thing. Our congresswoman came out on our side. Still nothing from Aqueduct."

"I'll tell you," Bernina said, "the silence from that corporation and the state water board made the community edgy. Talk of the water grab got ugly in the Deluxe Billiards, our one nontourist saloon. People's tempers rose. Some folks suggested that if the application was granted, there would be nasty repercussions. They speculated on what kind of rifle would be best suited to take out a water bag, and which tools would rupture pipe. Others talked about how easily a pumping station far upsteam in the woods could be vandalized."

Curtis spoke for the first time. "Folks

around here own a lot of guns, and they aren't afraid to use them."

"Use them too damn often to settle their disputes," Jane White commented.

Joseph decided to steer the conversation away from that tack; to his way of thinking, Bernina talked entirely too much about possible violent solutions to their problems. "In December," he said, "Aqueduct completed the application process and contacted us. Their CEO, Gregory Erickson, proposed that they come here this month and float one of the bags, so we could see for ourselves how they'd look, and be reassured that they'd have no adverse effect on the appearance of the coast. And he offered to answer any and all questions at a community forum. Something about his proposal sounded suspicious: none of the shoreline here is public property. Where, we asked him, was he going to float the bag? And that's when the other shoe dropped. Timothy McNear was going to give them access to the land the old mill stands on. And not just for demonstration purposes, either. When the state water control board granted their petition — *when*, Erickson said, not if — McNear had promised them the right to trench and lay pipe across the mill site."

Joseph had been over this ground so many times before that he could recount what had happened without engaging either his brain or his emotions. Now he was surprised to find himself becoming angry. Surprised to hear the strong vibration in the voice that, for his whole career, he'd used to rouse crowds to action. Since his departure from Sacramento and return to his childhood home, he'd more or less just been going through the motions, but on the eve of the public forum, he found himself really caring again. Maybe, he thought, the old fires were not dead after all.

Jenna Longways said, "Jane wrote a press release so we could break the story statewide. Newspapers and TV stations finally took notice. Joseph convinced us of the advantage of bringing Erickson to town for the forum, and urged the Friends to accommodate him. And when your foundation" — she nodded at Jessie and Fitch — "offered their assistance, he decided to take them up on it."

Jessie said, "Once you accepted our offer, things happened fast at the foundation." She looked at Collier, whose gaze was once again wandering around the restaurant, and Joseph thought he detected an impatient twitch at the corner of her mouth before she went on. "Fitch, who's the most recent addition to the panel of attorneys we call on for expert assistance, agreed to take on the project within twenty-four hours. And I received the assignment the next day. The foundation's researchers worked overtime to prepare the files we'd need, and . . . well, here we are."

Steph came up behind Joseph and spoke in a low voice. "Gregory Erickson's assistant just called. Asked Kim for a table for four. If I'd answered the phone, I'd've put them off till you people were gone, but she told them to come ahead."

Joseph sighed. "Not much to be done about it, then, is there? But I wouldn't expect trouble. They're southerners — polite people. And we've been known to behave, too."

"Most of you."

He followed the direction of her dark gaze, along the table to Curtis.

"Let me handle him." He stood and put a reassuring hand on her shoulder, feeling her long dark curls brush the back of his fingers. Quickly he moved away and went to stand beside Curtis's chair.

Curtis looked up. "What?" he said.

"The waterbaggers have reserved a table. They'll be here shortly."

"And you're gonna tell me to make nice."

"Now's not the time for a confrontation, friend."

"It damned well should be the time. For the Perdido. And for our people."

Our people.

Joseph realized that by the phrase, Curtis did not mean the Pomos as a whole, but only the hundred or so tribespeople who claimed as their own sixty acres of land tucked deep in the hills above Oilville. And the irony behind the word "our" was not lost on him.

Curt, he knew, had found many reasons to put distance between them, the most convenient of which was Joseph's turning his back on the collection of trailers and prefabs and rusting Quonset huts that they'd once both called home. Joseph was neither proud nor regretful of his defection, but it had given Curt a reason to hate him. Now he wondered about the connection Curt had made between the Perdido and the Pomos, since the river did not run through tribal lands. Spiritual, he supposed.

He said, "Don't give them the edge they need, Curt."

The door of the restaurant opened, and heads turned as Gregory Erickson and his administrative assistant, Neil Woodsman, stepped inside. Two other people, whom Joseph hadn't seen before, followed.

Erickson ignored the hostile looks directed toward them by most of the diners as he surveyed the room. He was what Joseph thought of as a typical upper-class southerner: slender, with prominent teeth, high cheekbones, a pale complexion, and a rapidly receding hairline. He and the two men behind him appeared agitated. Woodsman — sandy haired, bearded, and stocky — looked calmer as he stared at the Friends' table. In seconds all four started toward it.

Curtis stood, tossing his napkin on the table, and Joseph braced himself to restrain him. The waterbaggers stopped a few feet away from them, Erickson placing his hands on his hips and leaning forward belligerently.

"Which one of you bastards did it?" he demanded.

Joseph tensed, felt Curt go taut beside him. Lee Longways's chair scraped on the floor as he rose.

"What seems to be the problem?" Joseph asked.

"As if you didn't know!"

Erickson's face darkened with anger. Joseph glanced at Woodsman, was surprised to see him wearing a look of wry amusement.

"I have no idea what you're talking about," Joseph said.

"Well, somebody in this place does!"

"If you'd calm down and explain —"

"You want explanations?" Erickson's voice became shrill. "Come on over to the motel and see for yourselves!"

He whirled and headed toward the door. Woodsman shrugged and motioned for Joseph and Curtis to precede him. As one, Curtis and the others in their party followed. Erickson was striding well ahead, but he stopped on the highway's shoulder as a semi sped past, blasting on its horn. Then he ran across the pavement.

"What the hell's the matter with him?" Curt said.

Joseph didn't hazard a guess.

Erickson had reached the far end of the parking lot by the time the rest of them crossed the highway. Two white midsize cars stood there, and even at a distance Joseph could read the graffiti spray-painted on them.

WATERBAGGERS OUT — OR ELSE!
NO WATER GRAB!
FUCK YOU!

The first two were slogans of the Friends'

protest campaign. The latter, Joseph thought, was less than original but fit well in a small space.

As they drew closer, he saw that the two front tires of each car were flat. Erickson was in a full-blown rage now, marching around the cars and flailing his arms as he pointed at them. "One of you did this; I know you damn well did!"

Joseph made a calming gesture. "Mr. Erickson —"

"You couldn't work things out in a civilized manner; no, not a bunch of hicks like you. I won't stand for threats and intimidation. I won't!"

Neil Woodsman stepped forward. "Gregory —"

"Shut up! Just shut up and call the sheriff! I want these people arrested. All of them." Erickson stalked off toward one of the motel units.

Woodsman stood staring after him. "Off his meds," he muttered to one of the other Aqueduct personnel.

"Jesus," Bernina said, "this guy heads a big corporation?"

"Well, they *are* rental cars," Jenna Longways told her. "Nobody wants to deal with something like this."

"Yeah," her husband said, "but that

boy's got a severe anger-management problem."

Woodsman turned on him, eyes narrowed.

To avoid any further conflict, Joseph reached into his pocket for his cell phone and held it out to Woodsman. "Call nine-one-one and get the sheriff out here."

Steph Pace

Steph shut down the computer and pushed back from the desk, took off her reading glasses and rubbed her tired eyes. Another day's accounts balanced, the receipts in the bag for night deposit. Through the wall between her tiny office and the kitchen, she could hear the dishwasher groaning. Soon Tony Tomasini, bartender and jack-of-all-trades, would bang the back door on his way out, and then she would be alone.

What a day! First Timothy McNear's inexplicable appearance. Then she'd found that the tomatoes had been omitted from her produce order. Kat Puska had called in sick before the dinner service, leaving her twin sister, Kim, to deal with the customers, so Steph had filled in. And finally there had been the confrontation with the waterbaggers.

Gregory Erickson's lack of control had surprised her. During his two previous visits to the restaurant, his demeanor — and that of his staff — had been low-key, as if they wished to avoid any potential conflict with the townspeople. But the damage to their rental cars, which the sheriff's deputies seemed to consider a teenage prank, had really set Erickson off.

Another surprise was Curt's behavior. She'd expected him to respond to Erickson's accusation with in-your-face belligerence, but he hadn't. Joseph's calming influence, probably. Even after all these years of estrangement he had that power over Curt. Decades-old ties bound them — bound her as well. Ties like the filaments of a spider web, allowing some movement but never enough to break free.

She didn't want to think about that now, although she'd done little else since Joseph's return to the Cape. Seeing him on a near daily basis brought back the past in ways that her sporadic encounters with Curt didn't.

Nearly midnight by the ship's clock on the wall. She should go home to bed in order to be fresh for tomorrow's breakfast service. But the dream-troubled nap she'd caught late this afternoon had been a mistake; it would surely rob her of sleep for hours. She got up, put on her coat, and made her nightly security check. Outside, she walked the block to the bank and put the deposit bag in the slot. Then, instead of returning to where her car waited at the restaurant, she continued north to the public beach access at Cauldron Creek.

The creek was so named because it emptied into a deep wave-carved basin where, at high tide, the water roiled about, tossing the stones that were trapped there to the surface and creating the illusion of bubbles. It was low tide now, and Steph picked her way down a steep trail and through the debris at the bottom of the basin, then climbed the sandbank on the far side. Across the beach the surf lapped placidly, making a soft shushing sound. Steph turned north again, away from the winking lights of town.

A steady offshore breeze tousled her curls, bringing with it a strong and vaguely unpleasant odor from the kelp beds. The cliffs curved ahead of her, dark and rugged, spilling down in huge, jagged slabs to meet the sand. At an outcropping that had always reminded her of a crouching prehistoric creature, she stopped, catching the smell of cigarette smoke. She peered into the shadows, saw an orange tip glow and then fade.

"Hey, Steph." Curt's raspy voice.

"Hey, there."

"Come join me?"

Now she could make him out, seated halfway up the creature's humped spine. She hesitated before replying, having no desire to join him or anyone else, then said, "Why not?" and scrambled up beside him.

"Smoke?" Curt asked when she was settled, her back against the rough ledge.

"No, thanks."

"Gave it up, huh?"

"That and a lot of other things."

He didn't respond, but she saw his eyes glitter as he drew on his cigarette.

"How come you're not at the Friends' meeting?" she asked.

"They don't need me. They got their New Yorkers now."

"You think those people can turn this situation around?"

Curt shook his head. "Nah, they came in too late. Don't see how they can pull a convincing case together in time for the hearing. Not that the lawyer the Friends hired was doing so good, either. I'm afraid tomorrow's our last battle, and it's gonna be a bloody one."

"You're expecting more trouble, then?"

"Yeah. But I'm not gonna manufacture any, if that's what you're thinking. Joseph warned me against giving the waterbaggers an edge that they can use against us. Too damn bad whoever tagged those cars didn't think about that."

"Kids."

"Probably — although I wouldn't put it past some adults in the community."

"Who?"

"Nobody specific, just the good-ol'-boy contingent."

A silence grew between them. Curt smoked and stared out to sea. When a wave boomed at the end of the outcropping, Steph started.

"You're jumpy," Curt said.

"Yeah."

"You want to talk about it?"

"No. Yes. Curt, d'you ever think . . . about that night?"

Silence, and then he shifted on the hard stones. "I think about it."

"We've never talked —"

"We haven't talked since then."

"Come on, we see each other —"

"Haven't talked about anything that matters, I mean."

"Has Joseph ever . . . ?"

"Joseph?" A bitter laugh, and he tossed his cigarette away.

"He —"

"Look, Steph, let it lay." Curtis pushed to his feet. "It's cold here. You coming?"

She shook her head and watched his cat-like descent from the outcropping to the sand.

Let it lay.

Close that can of worms and keep it closed.

Easy advice to give, maybe. Not so easy to follow.

Timothy McNear

At close to midnight Timothy could still see the delineation between sea and sky. It was faint, merely a matter of different shades of darkness, but his practiced eye focused and held on it. Lately he'd taken to staying in the loft, swaddled in his big chair, neglecting to eat the dinner the housekeeper had left for him in the oven, sipping one more glass of Scotch than was advisable.

Waiting.

For what?

Death? No. In spite of the arthritis and shortness of breath after he climbed the ladder, he was in good shape, and longevity ran in his family.

Forgiveness? Not much chance of that. He'd long ago given up on receiving a phone call from his estranged son or grandsons. He'd hoped one day to see understanding in Stephanie Pace's eyes, but now that he'd betrayed not only her trust but everyone else's, he knew it would never happen.

Since that betrayal, the morning light,

which used to greet him like an old friend, seemed cold and alien. The ring of the phone and the knock at the door, or any of the other things normal people expected and welcomed, didn't happen. He was and would forever be alone, reduced to listening to his own heartbeat and staring at the horizon.

Alone, and waiting.

For what?

Saturday, February 21

Jessie Domingo

Jessie finished the last of her fish-and-chips, tossed the cardboard container in a trash barrel, and went to stand at the railing of the deck behind the Blue Moon Cafe. The morning had dawned sunny and clear, except for some clouds piled on the horizon that the local weather forecast had said were part of a storm front that was due to move in that evening. The Pacific was a brilliant blue and placid; sea lions sunned themselves on the offshore rocks or glided through the waves in sinuous motion. Jessie watched one climb onto an overhanging shelf, displacing two others, who bellowed indignantly.

The town that had seemed so drab and shabby to her the day before now struck her as charming and somewhat festive. People streamed in and out of the café, the general store, and the other businesses, and wandered along the shoulders of the highway. They called out greetings to one another and stood talking in little groups; total strangers smiled at her as she made her way back to the motel. The fine weather had brought out the best in Cape Perdido, and Jessie was beginning to understand why people lived here in spite of its remoteness and lack of the amenities she was used to.

She went to the door of Fitch's unit, knocked, and once again got no response. The attorney had been absent from his room for over an hour, and it was nearly time for the public forum at the site of the defunct lumber mill to begin. She didn't intend to wait around for him and risk missing it. Let him find his own transportation.

She got into the rental car Joseph Openshaw had waiting at the motel for them, drove out of the lot, and followed the highway south from town, through a series of downhill switchbacks that brought it to sea level. The shore was lined with wind-warped cypress trees, and beyond them lay a sand beach. Offshore, more of the rock formations that Bernina Tobin had called sea stacks towered above the water. A long bridge spanned the Perdido River, wide at that point and blue as the sky, dividing around a small tree-dotted island, then merging several hundred yards before it flowed into the sea.

Early that morning Bernina had taken Jessie and Fitch on a tour of the lower

Perdido, parking in a graveled area at the north end of the bridge and leading them along a trail that wound for half a mile among tanbark oaks and pines, then forked, one branch descending to a pebbled beach. The river was swollen from the winter rains, rushing around boulders and carrying tree limbs and other debris. They had the beach to themselves except for a man tossing a ball to his Irish setter, which frolicked in the shallows.

"In a couple of months, this beach'll be crowded with people and dogs," Bernina told them. "A kayak-rental van sets up at the parking area and does a good business. By midsummer, the water's a lot lower, lazier. By fall, sandbars make it barely navigable. Add to that thousands of acre-feet of water being siphoned off annually, and recreational use'll drop off sharply."

She then led them back to the main trail and farther upstream, where the forest thickened and the ground was carpeted in pine needles and moss. At an outcropping above another beach, she stopped and pointed. "That's where they want to put their damn pumping station. They'd bury a cistern housing a series of electric pumps in the river channel and run a twenty-four-inch pipe down the stream and across

Timothy McNear's land to bags moored offshore. The pumping station would be unmanned except for periodic maintenance, and you can imagine the potential for vandalism that kind of situation poses."

At the Friends' meeting the previous evening, Bernina had speculated at length about additional vandalism or outright violence against the waterbaggers, but as Jessie stood in this quiet, beautiful spot, it seemed an unlikely prospect. But then someone had spray-painted the waterbaggers' cars, and she supposed Bernina, as part of the community, was in a much better position to judge its emotional climate than she.

Now, as she drove toward the defunct lumber mill, Jessie decided she'd work the crowd after the presentation, conduct an informal public opinion poll. Although the local level of hostility toward the waterbaggers would not be a large factor in the state board's decision, it could very well sway some of its members to the environmentalists' side.

Ahead the land curved out onto a point that formed a natural harbor, and on it she spotted the long beige buildings of the old mill, rust-streaked smokestacks rising high above them. The car in front of her braked and pulled onto the shoulder; seeing that the roadside ahead was lined with vehicles, Jessie did the same. As she joined a group of people who moved slowly toward the mill, she listened to snatches of their conversations.

". . . bastards think they can just come in here and take our water, they got another think comin'!"

"The tugs they're gonna tow those bags with, they're slow, gotta keep close in so they don't clog up the shipping lanes. Could scare off the humpbacks when they migrate. That'd be the end of the whale-watching business."

"Yeah, and those bags're gonna be seven hundred and seventy feet long. Can you believe it? That's two and a half football fields!"

"And a football field wide. Don't forget that."

"Well, I'm gonna hear what the man's got to say, but it's not gonna change my mind."

"Old Timothy McNear — remember all his talk about tearing down the mill and making it a park with public access to the ocean? What a liar!"

"You seen that southern guy? He looks shifty as all get-out."

That southern guy: Gregory Erickson, CEO of Aqueduct Systems. Jessie wouldn't have called him shifty, not exactly, but her impression of him the night before had been off-putting — an impression bolstered by the man's vague and confusing background.

Erickson, one of the foundation's researchers had learned, was a native of the Raleigh-Durham area. He had a degree from an Atlanta business college that was little more than a diploma mill, but the résumé he'd submitted along with his application to the state water board listed an impressive number of jobs in "resource management" with firms throughout the world. However, when the researcher attempted to contact the companies regarding Erickson's tenure, he'd come up with either blanks or resistance. Only Erickson's last position, as a public relations specialist for an Australian firm that harvested water in Turkey, was fully verifiable, but even there the specifics were sketchy. Apparently he'd picked up enough expertise and capital during his tenure with those firms to establish Aqueduct Systems and had been in business for three years, in partnership with a consortium of Japanese and South American investors.

The company had completed successful water harvesting projects in Eastern Europe, and Cape Perdido was to be its first foray onto American soil. Had Erickson not been involved in the consortium, the situation would have been somewhat straightforward, but those foreign interests made it tricky —

"You're a pretty lady."

Jessie started and looked at the speaker, a small, nut brown man with a bad limp, wearing a blue knitted cap with an absurdly large dirty-white tassel. He smiled crookedly, revealing yellowed teeth. "Yes, ma'am, very pretty."

". . . Thank you."

"You going to the festivities? I am. Officially, it'll be my first time inside the mill since they shut it down. D'you mind if I walk with you? What's your name?"

The man was strange and smelled of alcohol, but seemed harmless enough. "Jessie."

"Jessie. That's a pretty name. I'm Harold. Not Hal, I don't like Hal. Or Harry. Just call me Harold."

"I'm glad to meet you, Harold."

"Thanks. Oh, look, they're all waiting at the gate!"

Two green and white cruisers from the

Soledad County Sheriff's Department were pulled up across a wide gate in the high chain-link fence that surrounded the mill, and officers stood guard, waiting till it was time for the public to be admitted. A TV van that Jessie had seen at the motel was parked near the cruisers, and a man from the county station was videotaping the protesters. They congregated to the left side, wearing large plastic buttons that read, "Don't Drain the Perdido!" and holding hand-lettered signs. Jessie could hear them chanting: "No water bags, no water grab . . ."

"They're all waiting," the little man added, "just like we waited when Mr. McNear shut down the mill. We waited with our signs, and we sent in a petition, but he shut it down anyway, and that was that."

"You worked there?"

"Oh, yes. I was a sawyer till I had my auto accident — busted up my leg and hip pretty bad — and they gave me a desk job. Made me timekeeper; I worked with young Mack Kudge. He was my part-time assistant after school let out. Wonder what Mack would think of all this going on at our mill? Not that it makes no never-mind to him anymore."

"Who?"

But the man was distracted. "Oh, balloons!" he exclaimed.

Jessie looked where he was pointing, saw a flock of bright green and white spheres rising into the sky above the protesters. When she glanced back, the odd little man was gone.

She continued moving with the crowd until it came to a halt near the sheriff's-department cruisers; then she weaved through it toward the protesters. Bernina Tobin, wrapped in a red cape and multicolored skirt, was there, along with other members of the Friends whom Jessie had met at last night's meeting, but their ranks had been swelled by dozens. They wore all-weather gear, jeans, and sturdy boots; many had the toughened skin of people who worked outdoors. A man in a wheelchair held a sign that read, "Disabled Vets for the River." A woman with cotton-candy pink hair and flowing robes to match was blowing soap bubbles. One of the bubbles touched Jessie's cheek before it burst.

Bernina grabbed her arm. "Look at this! Will you just look at all these people who've come out in support of us!"

"It's going better than planned, isn't it?"

"Well, I was a little concerned when the deputies let in a car containing Timothy

McNear and the waterbaggers a while ago." She glanced around. "Some of these folks're here to look for trouble — men, of course, who else? — but the deputies'll keep them in line."

Jessie followed Bernina's gaze to a group of men who were leaning on an old, mud-splattered Jeep that was pulled onto the shoulder on the opposite side of the highway. They were drinking beer and making unintelligible comments to passersby.

"Good old boys," Bernina added bitterly. "The kind who think a show of arms in the parking lots of the bars is the perfect end to a Saturday night."

One of the men yelled, "Let's go, guys!" He crushed his beer can, hurled it into the roadside ditch, then led the others across the highway. They pushed into the waiting throng, jostling and shoving and receiving irritated looks in response.

"Assholes," Bernina said. "The world would be better off if men had never been invented."

Jessie had occasionally voiced similar sentiments — hadn't every woman? — but she decided not to feed into Bernina's intense prejudice.

"Where's Joseph?" she asked.

"Inside, at the podium. I asked him to do the honors; he's a better speaker than me." Bernina glanced at her watch. "Almost time."

There was a stirring at the front of the crowd, and people stepped back as two deputies got into their cars and edged the wheels off the access road. Another pair rolled back the gates. Slowly the crowd moved forward, the protesters allowing most of them to pass before bringing up the rear. In spite of the wintery temperature, the sun made Jessie overly warm. She pulled off the hood of her parka and let the strong, cold sea wind stream through her hair. It brought with it the odors of brine and creosote. The broken-asphalt road led past a boarded-up guard station and between two of the mill's long buildings, which slumped under sagging roofs, their paint pitted, high windows broken. Graffiti covered their walls; obviously the chainlink fence was no deterrent to local taggers, and if McNear employed guards, they were grossly ineffective.

The road went up a rise where corrugated-iron sheds fanned out to either side, then descended toward the shoreline. At its top Bernina stopped and motioned at the scene below.

75

A wide concrete pier extended into the water at the end of the road, and a wooden platform had been erected at its base; several folding chairs and a stand with two microphones were arranged on it. The sea was choppy here, and a red and white tugboat tied up beside the pier bobbed and strained at its moorings. A high, elongated royal blue mass floated at the pier's end like the carcass of a giant sea creature, nearly filling the crescent-shaped harbor.

"My God," Jessie said, "is that the bag?"

Bernina nodded grimly. "Inflated to its full size with seawater. And Erickson thinks it isn't an eyesore!"

"Eyesore" was putting it mildly. As Jessie had overheard someone in the crowd say, the bag was more than two and a half football fields long, at least a third that wide, and some ten feet high. It dwarfed the pier, extending far along the point to the northern boundary of the mill property. Its blue color looked unnatural against the sea.

"Erickson claims the bags'll blend in when they're anchored offshore," Bernina said.

"They'd have to be halfway to Japan to blend in."

"Exactly. And Erickson knows that. He's

a typical product of a capitalistic, patriarchal society — blind to everything but his profit margin. When I think this land was supposed to become a public park after Timothy McNear razed the mill, I could just spit nails! What kind of recreational facility would that be, with a tug belching exhaust, and a big blue bag wallowing offshore?"

"Any idea why McNear agreed to support the waterbaggers' project?"

"Sheer meanness, according to people who know him. And money, of course. They must've paid him well."

Bernina started down the rise, and Jessie followed. As they neared the platform, she saw Joseph Openshaw mount its steps, followed by Gregory Erickson. A few moments later they were joined by the two other Aqueduct people she'd seen in the restaurant the night before and Neil Woodsman. Woodsman remained by the steps, holding out his hand to a tall white-haired man in a tan trench coat. The man ignored it and mounted the steps slowly, taking the chair that Erickson offered.

"Timothy McNear," Bernina said. "The traitor himself."

Jessie studied McNear. Her files said he was in his mid-seventies, but his appearance was that of a much younger man. His white hair was luxuriant, his relatively unlined face a deep saltwater tan, his carriage erect. As he sat, his eyes scanned the crowd as if he were searching for someone. Then he looked away, focusing on Gregory Erickson.

Erickson had dressed for the occasion in a blue plaid shirt whose color exactly matched that of the water bag. Coincidence? Jessie suspected not. The CEO stood in conference with Joseph Openshaw for a moment, then sat as Joseph went to the podium and took one of the microphones from its stand. After the usual grunts and whines from the sound system, he spoke into it, and the crowd quieted.

"Good afternoon. I'm Joseph Openshaw of the Friends of the Perdido, and the gentleman to my right is Gregory Erickson, CEO of Aqueduct Systems. Mr. Erickson has offered to meet with us today to discuss his company's proposal to export water from the Perdido to southern California."

As Joseph went on to outline the basic plan — hardly necessary for this crowd — Jessie felt a tap on her shoulder. Fitch Collier's angry voice said, "Where the hell have you been? You took the car, and I had to bum a ride down here with a stranger."

She turned to him, saw his mouth was

white and pinched. His blue eyes glittered in anger behind his tinted lenses. Cell phone withdrawal, perhaps?

"I could ask you the same," she said. "I checked your room starting around noon, and you weren't there."

"Well, why didn't you wait for me?"

"I went to the general store and picked up a sandwich for lunch, and then I —" Why was she explaining herself to him? "I didn't want to be late for this —"

"Sssh!" someone behind them said.

Gregory Erickson had risen and taken the second microphone. Joseph said, "Before we throw this open to a general question-and-answer session, Mr. Erickson, I have a few questions that have been submitted in writing. The first is mine. You're proposing to take water for free from the Perdido — a river held in the public trust — and sell it for profit. Do you consider that a moral act?"

The philosophical nature of the question seemed to perplex Erickson, and for a moment he hesitated. Then he said, "To address the issue of our taking the water for free, it will not be without cost to us. Construction of the pumping station upstream, sinking of the pipeline into the alluvium within the riverbed, acquiring the bags, contracting with the tugboat companies — these are expensive propositions."

Joseph asked, "What is the estimated cost to get this project up and running?"

"That depends on the variables. Until we get a project under way, we have no idea what those variables may be."

Sidestepping the questions, Jessie thought. No consideration for the moral issue. And no one goes into a project of this size without accurate cost estimates.

Openshaw seemed to be thinking the same thing; he smiled ironically as he said, "I see. Now let's address the first part of my question: Is this a moral project?"

Erickson frowned. "When approved, the project will be in compliance with all local, state, and federal laws. It will be in compliance with all international laws and precedents."

"But the underlying morality — ?"

"Some of us call what he wants to do stealing!"

The loud voice came from the back of the crowd. Jessie turned, saw a heavyset, red-faced man in an olive drab parka — one of the group who had been drinking on the other side of the highway. From under his matching cap, wiry blond hair protruded in big tufts.

Erickson flushed and looked at Neil Woodsman; quickly Woodsman stood and took the microphone from him. His motions were leisurely and self-assured, his face unperturbed. In a deep baritone whose accent was British rather than southern, he asked, "Is it moral to allow municipalities less fortunate than yours to die of thirst?" His tone was openly patronizing.

"Nobody down there's dyin' of thirst," the red-faced man shouted, "they're usin' the water to grow their lawns and wash their cars and fill their swimming pools!"

The man's companions clapped and stomped and whistled. Another man yelled, "Right on, Ike!"

Joseph intervened. "Let's move on to the next question —"

Fitch called out, "I have one."

"Mr. Collier?"

"Mr. Woodsman, what is the role of Marco Candelas, of Rio de Janiero, Brazil, in your operation?"

"He is a partner in the consortium of which we are a member."

"And what is that consortium called?"

"Galactic Water, Limited."

Jessie glanced at Fitch, saw he was smiling thinly. "Oh, and do you intend to eventually export water to Mars?"

Woodsman scowled at the gibe, and Fitch said, "Question withdrawn. Now, what is the role of Hiroshi Okamodo, of Osaka, Japan, in your operation?"

"He is a partner in the consortium."

"And Jesus Mondragon, of Buenos Aires, Argentina?"

"He is also a partner."

"And your position with Galactic Water is . . . ?"

"Also a partner, and chairman of the board."

Now Jessie saw where Fitch was going with this. Erickson's involvement with foreign nationals was one of the key points in the arguments Fitch would set forth before the state board; by bringing it out in the open now, he hoped to further rally the public against the water grab, as well as warn Aqueduct — perhaps in the slim hope that they would withdraw their application — that he planned to use this point against them.

"So," he went on, "if the state of California's water resources control board grants rights to extract water from the Perdido to Aqueduct Systems, it would essentially be granting such rights to you as sole owner of the firm and also as a principal in Galactic Water?"

"That is correct."

"Then it would require only an administrative change to transfer title to these rights to one of the other partners in Galactic Water?"

". . . I suppose so." Now Woodsman looked to Erickson for assistance.

"And if such title were transferred, the project would then be regulated under the North American Free Trade Agreement or the World Trade Organization, thus allowing you to circumvent California law."

"What the *hell* does all that have to do with this asshole comin' in here and ruinin' our river?" The red-faced man again.

More whistles, claps, and shouts. The point Fitch was trying to make apparently didn't interest the man and his friends. He went on. "We don't need some guy from North Carolina messing with the Perdido, and if he tries to —"

Whump!

The percussive sound drowned out the report of the first shot. Jessie started and looked around frantically. The crowd was momentarily silent; then people began shouting and milling about in panic when they heard a second shot ring out. Jessie ducked down, pulling Fitch, who had frozen, along with her.

A third shot. Now people were rushing

along the access road toward the highway, shoving and trampling one another. Through the microphone, Joseph yelled for everybody to keep calm. Jessie raised her head, saw he was the only person left on the platform. The others were scrambling into two cars parked near the pier.

A sheriff's cruiser inched through the gate, parting the panicky crowd, then bumped off the pavement and sped overland in the direction from which the shots had come. The car carrying the waterbaggers and McNear moved quickly up the access road, causing cries of protest from those it nosed aside. Jessie looked around to see if anyone had been hit, and saw the TV cameraman frantically filming the giant water bag. It spouted like a humpback whale.

Someone had decided that vandalism and verbal threats against Aqueduct International weren't enough.

Joseph Openshaw

"The shooter was probably on top of the old office building," the deputy, a man named Worth, told Joseph. "At least, we found a ladder leaning against the wall there. Newish one, aluminum, hadn't been exposed to much weather."

"Must've been a powerful weapon to make that big a hole in the water bag."

"Yeah, something like a thirty-aught-six, three rounds placed close together. Maybe we can recover the bullets from the bag, maybe not. Damn thing's gonna be a bitch to get out of the water."

"The tug —"

"Is trapped at the pier by the bag. We've got one hell of a mess on our hands."

Joseph felt someone come up beside him. Jessie Domingo, with Fitch Collier close on her heels. The lawyer hunched inside his expensive down parka, shivering. Domingo's jacket was thrown open to the wind, her cheeks rosy, her eyes bright.

Joseph said to the deputy, "Let me know when you've got something more." Then he turned to the others. "Quite an introduction you people're getting to our little community. How about we go have a drink?"

Jessie nodded, but Fitch shook his head. "I need to make some calls."

"Give you a ride back to the motel?"

"I'll take our rental car, if Jessie doesn't mind."

Jessie said, "I'll go with you, Joseph."

The Deluxe Billiards hadn't changed since its owner used to wink at Joseph and his high-school friends' false IDs. A horseshoe-shaped bar, two pool tables, small dance floor in front of the jukebox, tables with candles in red glass globes. Tourists who went looking for what passed for nightlife on the Cape generally ended up at the Oceansong, on the bluff north of town; the Deluxe, on a side street east of the highway, was strictly for locals.

Joseph watched as Domingo took in their surroundings. The Deluxe was, he supposed, about as different from her New York City hangouts as possible. But she didn't seem displeased, and took him up on his suggestion of a pale ale from a Calvert's Landing microbrewery. Then she sat back, seeming content for the moment to listen to a country song that was playing on the jukebox. Joseph glanced around the shadowy room, nodding to acquaintances: Marie and Tom Wallis, high-school sweethearts now married twenty years; Rosalind Katz, working on her third divorce and probably her fifth martini; Bob Alonzo, once the class cut-up and now superintendent of the west county unified school district. In the dim light, they didn't look all that much older than in the days when they'd flashed those fake IDs; if he closed his eyes and listened to the music, he could imagine that he was once again on the dance floor, Steph moving gracefully in response to his lead. . . .

Their beers arrived. Jessie tasted hers, nodded approval. Then she said, "I understand you're originally from this area."

"Born and raised in the hills above Oilville."

"The reservation?"

"It isn't officially a rez, although we call it that. Just sixty acres given to some tribal members by Timothy McNear's father in the nineteen-fifties. Their families had been living there and working the lumber camp since the mill was founded, and they'd always been good laborers, so before old man McNear gave Timothy control of the company, he signed over the deed." Joseph smiled ironically. "Not that it was much of a sacrifice; the land's poor, wasn't doing him any good."

"And you lived there till you went to Berkeley?"

"Yeah. Attended the unified schools, fished the Perdido, hunted in the hills. Raised a fair amount of hell up and down the coast. Didn't really appreciate the countryside back then. Like most of the kids around here, I was dying to get out. Wasn't until I was at Cal on scholarship that I came to realize what a wonderful natural world we have here."

"And that turned you into an ecologist?"

"I had a lot of help from a couple of my professors, but yes, I suppose so. Losing something will make you aware of how precious it is."

"Losing?"

Joseph hesitated, surprised to find himself talking so freely to this young woman. "In a sense. Berkeley, Sacramento, the other places I've been, have changed me. I come back now, I find I'm *from* here, but not *of* here." Enough said. "But what about you? Were you raised in New York?"

"Long Island. It's not so different there: the kids're all dying to get out, mainly to

Manhattan, which they consider the be-all and end-all."

"And so you did."

"Not exactly. My parents wanted me to see more of the world. Dad had traveled around a lot — he was a relief pitcher for the Mets."

"Oh, yeah? What's his name?"

"Kip Domingo."

"You know, I think I saw him pitch. I'm a big baseball fan."

"Not bad, was he?" Pride was evident in Jessie's voice. "He's a radio sportscaster now. And my mother, she acts — has for years — on a soap opera. Plays a real wicked-witch-of-the-west Scotswoman, which is funny, because while she actually is Scots, she's also the nicest person you could hope to meet. Anyway, it's a pretty grueling schedule, commuting to Manhattan five days a week. Like Dad, she wanted me to have more experience of the world before I decided where to settle. So they encouraged me to go to college at University of Colorado. That's where I got into environmental studies. As I told you yesterday, I read both your books. They're really good, and they helped shape my own philosophy."

"Thanks. You liked Colorado?"

"I loved it there."

"But you went back to New York."

"To work in state government, the department of environmental conservation. The job market was tough at the time, and a friend of Dad's had pull there. Anyway, I hated Albany. Absolutely hated it. The bureaucratic maneuvering, where you have to take two steps sideways to take one step forward." Momentarily her face clouded.

Something there that bothers her more than the usual disillusionment with state government. Wonder what?

Jessie shook her head, banishing the cloud, and went on. "Finally, six months ago, I heard about this job at ECC, applied, and actually got it. Not an easy thing; it's a very prestigious outfit. So now I live the Long Island girl's dream in the big city. It's fast-paced, exhilarating. Something going on every minute. And I love it there, too."

Joseph liked her unabashed enthusiasm. Liked the way her eyes shone and her cheeks flushed as she talked about her life. And reminded himself that she was young, too young for a tired veteran of the environmental — and various other — wars.

"Well," he said, "Cape Perdido must be quite a change from Manhattan."

"Yes." Jessie leaned forward, her face sobering as if she'd just remembered her purpose for being there. "Joseph, who do you think shot the water bag?"

He shrugged, unwilling to speculate just yet.

"That man heckling at the back of the crowd," Jessie went on, "who is he?"

"Ike Kudge."

A frown creased her high forehead. "Kudge . . . Does he have a relative named Mack?"

Now, where the hell had she heard that name? "Mack was his older brother."

"Was?"

"He died, years ago. Why do you ask?"

"A little man named Harold whom I met in the crowd mentioned his name. Said he used to work at the mill with him. And then he made a strange comment, about what was going on there making 'no never-mind' to Mack anymore."

So that was all. "The man you talked with is Harold Kosovich. He's the town eccentric — if a place like this can be said to have only one."

"He did seem a little . . . different. Tell me about him."

The subject of Harold Kosovich was infinitely preferable to Ike or Mack Kudge. "Harold lived in the trailer next to my

91

mother's when I was growing up, so I guess I'm used to him. He's part Pomo, part Russian, not that that has anything to do with him being strange."

"Pomo and Russian? Unusual combination."

"Not on the north coast. Fort Ross, down in Sonoma County, was established in the early eighteen-hundreds by Russian fur trappers, who came from Alaska with a group of Kodiak and Aleut Indians. The Pomos got on with the Russians — they were a damn sight more friendly than the Spanish or the white settlers — and traded with them. Eventually a number of them intermarried, and some even went back to Russia with the trappers when they pulled out of the area in the eighteen-forties. Harold's the grandson of one of the trappers who stayed behind."

"Did something happen to him, or has he always been this way?"

"I guess you could say life happened to him, but in a crueler way than it happens to most of us. His parents died when he was very young, and he was raised in a Catholic orphanage in Santa Rosa. I don't know if you're aware of what those places were like back then, especially for Indian kids, but he came out emotionally damaged. Arrested, a psychologist would say. Then he knocked around from place to place, working for the lumber companies. People who didn't understand him treated him badly; he drank too much — an old story. When he ended up here, working for McNear's, a few people on the rez, including my mother, took an interest in him, and he seemed to be getting better. Then the mill closed, and he lost everything that mattered to him. Now he's just a sad old man living out his life on Social Security and odd jobs. He's strange, but he's got a right to be."

"He seems fixated on the mill, on the past."

Joseph felt a stirring of annoyance at the statement. What did this young woman, who was living out her dreams, know about losing everything? But then, why should she, any more than Harold Kosovich should know about having the world at one's fingertips?

Jessie didn't seem to expect a reply. She sipped beer, gazed around moodily at the bar's other patrons. "I suppose," she said after a moment, "I should be getting back to the motel before Fitch comes looking for me. He's probably been on the phone to Eldon Whitesides."

"Oh? I didn't know Eldon was such a hands-on administrator."

"He isn't usually, but he's taking a special interest in the situation here."

"Why?"

She shook her head. "I guess because of the dangerous precedent that would be established if Aqueduct's application is granted."

In Joseph's opinion, Whitesides didn't give a rat's ass about precedent, unless it served to increase his stature and his stock portfolio.

"Of course," Jessie added, "Mr. Whitesides is something of a puzzle to all of us at ECC. No one really understands what motivates him."

And there you said a mouthful, young lady.

Steph Pace

Steph pulled away from the Calvert's Landing farmers' market, the back of her old Ford station wagon loaded with fresh produce. She'd spent over an hour making her selections from the stalls that were set up weekly in the high school parking lot, and she was eager to get back to the Cape before the major storm front that the morning forecast had predicted blew in. While most of what she bought for the restaurant was delivered by the wholesaler from the county seat at Santa Carla, she also liked to shop the independent sellers who turned out for the Saturday event.

Broccoli, she thought, turning north on Highway 1. Brussels sprouts and carrots and cauliflower and cabbages. All excellent vegetables, but no longer appealing after four long months of winter. Would spring ever come, bringing zucchini and green beans, peas and exotic greens? She was sick and tired of working with her cook on ways to make the old standbys interesting.

Or maybe she was just sick and tired, period.

After some miles, Green Valley Road appeared ahead and to the right, a black-topped secondary artery that snaked eastward through the hills. One quick turn, and in less than an hour she could be at its intersection with the 101 freeway. And then? North to Oregon, south to the Mexican border. Steph smiled as she pictured herself speeding toward a new life, tossing out winter vegetables as she went — free of the Blue Moon, free of Cape Perdido, and most of all, free of Joseph Openshaw.

There had been a time when the possibility of living without Joseph had been inconceivable. And later, a time when she had lived without him and been inconsolable. But there were many years after that when she'd scarcely thought of him, when months went by before a particular quality of the light, or color of the sea, or shape of a cloud formation caught her notice, and the words *Joseph would like that* sprang to her mind. Then, briefly, she'd be inconsolable once more.

Now, after twenty years, Joseph was back in her life, but he wasn't the man she'd once known. The relationship — too cool, too polite — wasn't the one they'd once had.

Don't speak of the past; forget everything we

ever were to each other. Old friends now, and that's all we can be.

His dictums, his parameters. Not hers.

The old Joseph, her Joseph, had vanished. No more wildness, no more passion. The new Joseph was a man who was merely going through the motions, and Steph, for the life of her, couldn't get through to him on any significant emotional level.

She was nearly to town, approaching the old mill, when she saw the sheriff's cruisers parked there and checked her watch. After four. Was the public forum still going on? She'd used the excuse of running errands and going to the farmer's market not to attend; large crowds — particularly ones that she feared would turn unruly — made her uncomfortable in the extreme. Besides, Joseph had dissected the potential water grab from every angle on those afternoons when he sat in her closed restaurant drinking cup after cup of coffee; nothing Gregory Erickson could say would have further informed her.

As she drew closer, she realized there were far too many sheriff's cars for simple crowd control. Two blocked the gate, and several more were drawn up along the fence. She spotted a familiar red pickup truck with a "Support Your Local Sheriff's Department" bumper sticker, and a big yellow Labrador retriever in the passenger's seat, and on impulse, pulled over.

Lester Worth, a deputy who frequently stopped for lunch at the Blue Moon, was the first person she encountered after she crossed the highway.

"Hey, Lester," she called, "what's happening here?"

Surprise creased his weathered face. "Steph! You don't know?"

"I've been down at the Landing. I saw Rho Swift's truck, figured something serious was going on." Rhoda Swift was the detective in charge of criminal investigations in the coastal area of the county.

"Serious for those water-grab people. Somebody shot up their bag." Lester leveled his index finger seaward, pulled back his thumb as if he were cocking a trigger. "Ka-boom! Three times. Murdered the thing."

"You don't seem very concerned."

He shrugged. "The way I see it, it was bound to happen. Maybe now they'll go away and leave us alone."

From what Joseph had told Steph about Gregory Erickson, the shooting would probably have the opposite effect. "You seen Rho?" she asked.

"She's down by the pier with the head waterbagger."

"Okay if I go look for her?"

"Be my guest."

Steph spotted Rhoda Swift halfway out on the pier, talking with Gregory Erickson. A massive royal blue form, puffy in places, flat and submerged in others, sloshed against the pilings, trapping the red and white tug that was moored there.

As Steph started along the pier, Erickson began waving his hands in the air, then spun on his heel and walked toward her in a tight, fast stride. As he passed, he glared. She kept going, to where the detective now leaned on the pier's railing, staring down at the remains of the bag.

"Hey, Rho," Steph said.

Swift turned. She was a small woman, in her late thirties. Curly black hair, grown longish since Steph had last seen her, framed her fine-boned face. "Hey, Steph," she replied. "Can you believe this? It's like a humpback swam into the harbor and died. Thank God it doesn't smell as bad."

"How the hell're you going to get it out of here?"

"Erickson's problem, or Timothy McNear's. Not ours."

Steph leaned on the railing next to Rho, and they regarded the bag in companionable silence. Steph had known the investigator since grade school, although not well, since she was a few years older than Rhoda. After Steph graduated from high school and Joseph deserted her for Berkeley, she had moved to Oregon for five years, and by the time she returned, Rho had gone off to Chico State. They'd run into each other occasionally after Rho joined the sheriff's department, and of course, Steph had heard the talk about her career difficulties and drinking and failed marriage; but by the time they connected again, while cochairing a Christmas toy drive sponsored by the sheriff's department and the Rotary Club, all that was behind Rho. Since then they'd become, if not friends, good acquaintances.

After a while Steph said, "You know who did this?"

Rho shook her head. "Shooter was over on the old administration building. Nobody saw — or admits to seeing — him. Frankly, I can't get too worked up over it."

"Erickson looked worked up."

"Well, sure. He thought he could show us the pretty blue bag and opposition to the water grab would automatically disappear.

This has told him he faces a fight." Rho paused. "I'd be derelict in my duty if I didn't ask if you know who did it."

"Me? Why . . . ?"

"Well, you're hooked in with the Friends of the Perdido crowd through Joseph Openshaw."

"You don't think they had anything to do with this? Or Joseph did?"

"I didn't say that. Besides, Joseph was on the platform when it happened. But it strikes me that he might've known or suspected what was about to go down."

"No, not possible. Joseph is strictly non-violent."

Rho was silent for a moment. "What about Curtis Hope? As I recall, he hasn't always been nonviolent."

"You mean the protests over Indian gaming in Rohnert Park last year? He wasn't part of the faction that got out of hand."

"I know that. I was thinking of his army service. He was a Ranger. Trained as a sniper."

"Really? Still, that was the army."

"Yeah, but it makes me wonder. He's got the ability to have done this" — she motioned down at the bag — "and snipers, they've always seemed a little creepy to me, even though I know it's a necessary job. I just thought he might've mentioned his military experience to you, given you a take on how he felt about it."

"We haven't really talked in a long time."

Rho straightened. "Okay, just thought I'd ask. If you hear anything, about anybody, you'll let me know, right?"

"Of course."

Rho nodded and started back down the pier, leaving Steph alone with a whole new set of suspicions and fears.

Timothy McNear

For the first time in over thirty years, he couldn't summon the desire or the strength to climb to the loft at the appointed time. Instead he sat with his drink at the table in front of the stone fireplace in the big kitchen, next to the French doors that overlooked the formal gardens. He hadn't turned on the outside spotlights, and could barely see the swaying fronds of the seventeen varieties of palms that his dead wife Caroline had collected from all over the world and nurtured here in the sunbelt above the sea.

The garden, three acres of exotic plantings, reflecting pools, and statuary, had been Caroline's refuge from their somewhat turbulent marriage; she'd spent hours working in it or in the little pagoda-style potting shed at its far reaches. Later, when his son and grandchildren lived with him, the shed became another kind of refuge: a fantasy world for two young boys who had lost their mother and been abruptly uprooted from their life in a comfortable suburb of San Francisco. Nowadays the garden was not exactly untended, but the dour part-time groundskeeper — one of a long succession Timothy had hired — neither cared for it nor took pleasure in it the way his wife and grandsons had.

Timothy rolled his glass between his long, slender fingers, acutely aware of the heavy silence. This house had never been a particularly happy or lively home, that he had to admit, but at least the voices of his family had filled it. But they were long gone, his wife and daughter dead, son and grandsons estranged. Twenty years since Rob had taken Max and Shelby away to Melbourne; longer than that since the boys had called up to him as he sat in his loft at sunset and he'd turned to see their small faces appear at the top of the ladder. . . .

It had grown dark in the kitchen, but he made no effort to turn on a light. After the debacle at the pier that afternoon, he wanted to hide like a dying animal. Better to *be* a dying animal — alone, resigned to the inevitability of its passing.

The palm fronds swayed outside the doors — gray on black, black on gray — as the storm front that had been predicted that morning moved in. Timothy watched and waited. The wind rose, baffling down the chimney, then spewing ash onto the hearth. The air grew chill and heavy.

After perhaps fifteen minutes, a figure appeared in dark silhouette at the edge of the garden. It paused there, also watching and waiting, then crossed toward the house. Timothy rose, went to the door, and opened it.

"I've been expecting you," he said.

Gregory Erickson stepped into the house, his mouth set grimly. "That business with our water bag being shot," he said. "You'd better not have been behind it, or there'll be hell to pay."

Jessie Domingo

Jessie was having a heated argument with Fitch, had just informed him that he was an arrogant son of a bitch for keeping her out of the loop where Eldon Whitesides was concerned, when the lights in her motel room flickered and suddenly went out.

Fitch said, "Whaaat?"

Wind blasted the front wall of the small unit; Jessie could feel its chill seeping in around the cheap aluminum frame of the window.

"Storm must've knocked out the power." She groped toward the switch by the door and flipped it to make sure. "Yeah, it's definitely out. Joseph warned me this might happen."

"Great! Just fucking great. Now what the hell do we do?"

"Call the office and ask for a flashlight?"

Over by the bed, Fitch stumbled around. There was a thump, and then he exclaimed, "Ouch! Dammit, where's the phone?" A clatter, and the bell tinkled as the instrument hit the floor. "Oh, hell!

This is impossible. Do something!"

Not two minutes before, he'd told her she was "peripheral" to his "mission." Now he was demanding her assistance.

"What do you suggest?"

"Help me find the . . . wait, here it is . . . oh, hell, I think I broke it." There was an undertone of panic in his voice now.

Was he afraid of the dark? "Look, it's no big deal. I'll walk down to the office —"

A knock at the door. Jessie called, "Come in."

The dark, heavyset woman who had registered them the previous afternoon stepped inside, her round face highlighted by the glowing kerosene lanterns she carried in either hand. "For you and Mr. Collier," she said, extending them to Jessie.

"Thanks very much, Ms. . . .?"

"Bynum. Nita Bynum. The kerosene, it'll last a couple of hours; storm should be over by then."

"Does the power go out often?"

"Every time there's a bad storm. You get used to it." She stepped out, shutting the door behind her.

"My God, Jess," Fitch said. He was standing by the bed, the wreckage of the phone at his feet. "You shouldn't tell just anyone who knocks to come on in. You don't know who it could be."

"This isn't New York, you know." She set one lantern on the table by her laptop, took the other to him.

"Have you forgotten there was a shooting today?"

"Of a water bag, not a person. And whoever did it is on our side."

"Not necessarily. This kind of country, they believe in violence for violence's sake. You've got to be more careful."

He was concerned, yes, but she sensed he was also trying to steer her away from the subject of Eldon Whitesides.

"Let's get back to what we were talking about," she said.

"*I* was talking; *you* were shouting."

"Why didn't you tell me that Eldon is in San Francisco, and coming here tomorrow?"

"He's not coming if this storm doesn't let up."

"Never mind the weather. What were you planning to do, wait till he arrived and then say, 'Oh, by the way, here's the boss'? And don't give me that crap about me being peripheral."

Fitch began inching toward the door. "Okay, maybe I was wrong not to tell you. And maybe what I said earlier was a little

. . . harsh. But you shouldn't have listened at my door while I was having a private phone conversation."

"I wasn't listening at your door. I was about to knock, and I overheard you talking with Eldon. The walls are paper-thin in this motel, in case you haven't noticed."

Fitch's hand was on the doorknob now. "Jess, I've apologized. Eldon decided to come out here after he heard about the shooting and —"

"He wouldn't've had time to get from New York to San Francisco since then."

Fitch was silent, trapped by his lie.

"Well?" she demanded.

"I'm not discussing this with you when you're behaving irrationally. Besides, I've got to meet with the hydrologist who's going to testify at the hearing, and I don't think you'd be an asset to our session. We'll talk in the morning." He went out, neglecting to latch the door, so it immediately blew open.

Jessie shut it, pressing the snap lock on the flimsy knob. Then she went over and picked up the phone. Its faceplate had popped off, but it still had a dial tone. She forced the plastic grid back over the push buttons, then sat down on the bed to consider this latest turn of events.

Before she'd left the Deluxe Billiards, she and Joseph had been joined by two women who were interviewing old-timers in connection with an oral history of Soledad County's coastal region. For an hour or so they'd been entertained with stories of the lumber booms in the doghole ports that used to dot the coast in the days before rail or truck transport. During Prohibition the ports, no longer in use for hauling lumber, became ports of call for trawlers laden with bootleg Canadian liquor. Jessie was so fascinated by the tales of the ongoing battle between the rumrunners and government agents that she lost track of the time, and it was nearly six when she hurried through the rain to the motel, hoping to collect Fitch and go to dinner at the Blue Moon. Above the rising wind, she'd heard Fitch's voice through the door.

"Where're you staying down there, Eldon? . . . The Four Seasons? Excellent hotel. And you'll fly up here on a charter tomorrow afternoon? . . . Good. I'm glad you could make the trip. The situation's heating up more quickly than we anticipated."

At that point Fitch's words became unintelligible. Jessie rapped on the door and stuck her head inside. Fitch frowned and motioned for her to leave. She mouthed that he should join her in her room when he was done on the phone.

She had to admit now that the beers she'd drunk at the Deluxe had made her less than tactful in questioning Fitch about Whitesides's visit, but his labeling her as "peripheral" and then telling her she wouldn't be an asset in his meeting with the hydrologist hadn't been diplomatic, either. In fact, it pointed out to her how badly in need of her services as a community liaison specialist he was. She sensed that Fitch's remoteness and faint air of condescension had already not endeared him to the people he'd met in Cape Perdido.

Okay, what was going on, anyway? Obviously, Whitesides had planned his visit to the Cape before this afternoon. Fitch had known he was coming. Why hadn't she? ECC was an efficient organization; whenever an employee traveled for the foundation, all the details of the trip were set down in writing, but there had been nothing about the director's plans in Jessie's information packet.

Outside, the rental car she and Fitch shared started up. She went to the window in time to see it turn north on the highway.

Didn't the hydrologist live to the south, in Calvert's Landing? Jessie located his number in her files, went to the phone, and dialed. No, the man told her, he had no plans to see Mr. Collier tonight. They had scheduled a breakfast meeting for eight the next morning.

So Fitch had lied to her not once but twice. Where had he gone?

Jessie sat down at the table, stared at the blank screen of her laptop, then at the flickering lantern. Dammit, everything was going wrong with a project at which she'd desperately hoped to succeed!

A couple of hours before, when she'd told Joseph Openshaw she was living her dream, she'd almost believed it. Scoring the job with ECC had been major, and she'd felt confident it was what she needed to get her career on track and prove herself. But now she had her doubts, and once again she felt a familiar, crushing disappointment.

Nothing I do is ever going to be good enough. Nothing.

Not true. What you mean is, you're never going to be Casey.

Casey Domingo, her smart, beautiful older sister. Casey, whom everyone, including Jessie, loved. Casey, who at thirty-two was cofounder and CEO of a successful software firm, a devoted wife and mother, on the boards of several philanthropic organizations, and being courted to run for city council of her Long Island town. One of those women who had it all.

Her whole life Jessie had heard people speak of her sister in awed tones: *She's the perfect daughter. She's the perfect sister . . . friend . . . wife . . . mother . . . businesswoman . . .*

And she'd heard the whispered corollary: *Too bad Jessie's not more like her. The girl's bright, but she's not living up to her potential.*

She'd tried; God knew she had. But she'd never done anything quite well enough.

Not that her parents had held unrealistic expectations for her or allowed their pride in her sister to overshadow their pride in Jessie's accomplishments. In fact, they were somewhat puzzled by the exacting and often frustrating standards she set for herself. No, as a therapist she'd consulted in college had pointed out, the burden to achieve was a self-imposed and unnecessary one.

But that knowledge didn't make it any lighter, or possible to put down.

One home run, that's all I need, and then maybe I can let go of this need to match up to Casey.

One home run — but I'm afraid I won't hit it here in Cape Perdido.

Joseph Openshaw

Joseph fought the wheel as the old van bounced through the ruts of the narrow, unpaved road. The wind buffeted the clumsy vehicle, and the rain came down too hard for the wipers to clear. He cursed himself for not yielding to his impulse to buy a heavy-duty pickup before moving back from Sacramento; at the time, he'd told himself the move was only temporary and the van would be adequate until he returned to the state capital. Now he knew that he was here in Soledad County for good. Stuck, end of the line.

His headlights showed a dark shape in the road, and he swerved, tires skidding on the mud. Tree branch, big one, and plenty more would come down in this storm. He was nuts to be out on a night like this, but at least he had come prepared: even after his years in the cities, he had not forgotten the time-honored local wisdom of always carrying your chain saw during the winter months.

He rounded a curve, avoiding a couple

of other branches, and then a horizontal row of orange reflectors on a board fence told him he was entering the rez. The power, on the same vulnerable grid as Cape Perdido, was out here, too. Familiar landmarks lay in darkness, but in his mind's eye he could see them: the Mallons' old Airstream trailer, the boarded-up prefab community center, the Quonset hut that housed the small store, the old, weathered barn. Nothing much had changed here since the days of his youth. He could find his way blindfolded.

He slowed to a crawl, peering through the windshield for the narrow lane that led to a collection of ramshackle houses and trailers. Turned onto it, drove to the end, and stopped. When he stepped out of the van, rain lashed at him. He hunched, pulling his denim jacket over his head, and ran through a grove of swaying pines to a single-wide that sat apart from the others, climbed its rickety steps to the door. No one answered his repeated knocks, and he saw none of the telltale flickering from oil lamps that he'd noted in the other dwellings' windows.

So Curtis wasn't home. What now? They'd never in their lives stood on formality — few on the rez did — but this was

Joseph's first visit here since his departure from Cape Perdido nearly two decades before. You didn't just walk into a man's home after all that time — certainly not into the home of a man like Curtis Hope.

A fresh gust of rain forced him to action. He walked in anyway.

The air inside the trailer was cold and damp. Joseph waited till he could pick out dim shapes, then groped toward the bar that separated the main room from the galley kitchen. In the days when Curt had lived here with his mother and father — both now deceased — the emergency lamps had been kept in the cabinet under the bar; Joseph doubted he'd moved them.

When he took one of the lamps out and lit it with the matches that were also stored there, he saw that Curt had made few alterations in the place. A patchwork quilt that his grandmother had sewn hung on the wall by the door; narrow metal bookcases contained paperbacks and knickknacks; the plaid couch and hulking sixties-style console TV were the same. He moved closer, looked at the titles on the bookshelves: romances and Westerns. The knickknacks were mainly ceramic cats. No, Curt hadn't changed a thing; it looked as if time had stopped for him with the death of his parents.

Joseph knew he should sit down to wait for his old friend's return, but curiosity drew him along the narrow hall to the bedrooms. The larger of the two was outfitted with a double bed covered in another quilt, and looked unused. The door to the other bedroom was shut; Joseph hesitated a moment, then pushed it open. A narrow iron bed, one Joseph remembered as being Curt's since childhood, stood against the far wall, made up with a woven blanket. The small, high window was draped with a heavy brown fabric. On the end wall hung a tapestry depicting a golden eagle; below it on a bureau lay a scattering of rocks.

Joseph moved closer and examined them. They were smooth and polished like those found in stream beds, arranged in a rough triangular shape, the top point toward the wall. He looked up, and the fierce eyes of the strangely lifelike eagle bored into his. The Pomos used most species as a source of food, but there were a number that were forbidden — the golden eagle because it was an extremely dangerous bird. Interesting that Curt had chosen to display this tapestry above what looked like rocks collected from the bed of the Perdido.

He backed out of the room and went down the hallway, his hand going automatically inside his jacket to the shirt pocket where he used to keep his cigarettes. It had been five years since he smoked, and the desire didn't come over him often, but when it did, it was strong and usually triggered by unease. He'd heard that Curt had developed an interest in the ways of their ancestors, but the display — call it a shrine — in the bedroom disturbed him.

He returned to the living room, sat down on a platform rocker that faced the door. Waited, feeling the damp and cold seep into his bones, listening to the rain beat on the flat roof. After more than an hour, he heard the growl of an engine, then the slam of a door. Footsteps approached and climbed the steps. The door flew open, hitting the wall and admitting a gust of wind. Curt's stocky figure filled the frame.

"What're you doing here, you son of a bitch?" he demanded.

"Waiting for you."

"Making free with my place, are you?"

"Too cold to sit in my van."

"So you just walked in."

"Always used to."

"That was before."

Curtis came inside, shut the door behind him. For a moment he stood still, then took off his slicker and tossed it onto the sofa. Sat down beside it, wary, hands braced on his knees. "What do you want, Joseph?"

"To talk about what happened this afternoon."

"The shooting? I'm talked out. Bernina, the others, they don't know where to go from here. They're waiting on you for guidance." He laughed harshly. "Guess they'll go on waiting."

"That's where you've been, with them?"

". . . Yeah."

"And where were you this afternoon?"

In the glow from the lamp he saw Curt nod. "So that's what this visit is about. Well, I wasn't on the roof of the admin building at the mill, if that's what you're thinking."

"You know who was?"

Curt was silent.

"Well?"

"Who appointed you my inquisitor?"

Joseph didn't reply.

"You know," Curt finally said, "I never thought it would come to this."

"What would?"

"Our friendship."

"We have a friendship? You couldn't prove it by me. I've been back, what? Seven, eight months? And this is the first time we've spoken in private."

"In order to speak, you need something to say."

"We have something to say now."

"No, Joseph." Curt shook his head slowly. "We don't."

"Look, I'm not going to judge you, but I need to know what's going on. If there's a problem, I'm here for you, just like I used to be."

"You weren't ever here for me. Or for Steph. Or Mack. And you're not here for Steph or me now. So get out and leave me alone."

"Curt —"

"Go away, Joseph."

What else could he do?

He went.

As he drove through the storm to Cape Perdido, Joseph reflected on what Curt had said. Maybe the reason his words hurt so much was because they were true.

Steph Pace

Her heart was pounding as she hurried along the moss-slicked path that wound through the palms, toward the stone wall at the edge of the property. Mist curled around the trees' trunks and dripped from their fronds, and the air lay very still. She was so intent on escape that it was some moments before she realized that the footsteps behind her had stopped.

She paused, her hand on one of the rough boles. Listened.

Silence.

She peered through the darkness to where the path curved at the statue of Kwan Yin.

No one there.

Now the flesh at the back of her neck rippled. One second he'd been close on her heels; then, before she knew it, he was gone. As if he'd been plucked up by some large, invisible hand.

Go back? Keep going, and hope they'd connect later? Maybe he knew another way out of here and had opted for it? But why would he leave her . . . ?

The canvas bag in her right hand was heavy. She shifted its long straps onto her shoulder.

Go on? Go back?

Go on. Hurry!

She turned and ran clumsily along the path to the wall — and safety. As she climbed it, she heard a shot —

A bright light flashed, instantly bringing Steph awake. The bedside lamp, left on to signal the end of the power outage, rescued her from the dark landscape of the dream. The old dream again, as ever, with not a detail altered.

She pushed up and squinted at the clock. Quarter to midnight. She couldn't have dozed off for more than fifteen or twenty minutes, yet the dream, like the actual experience it replicated, had seemed to go on for hours. And before that —

A banging at the door. She struggled from the bed, reached automatically for her robe, realized she still had it on. As she hurried down the hall of her small frame cottage, shreds of the fear that had enveloped her in sleep still clung to her. She fumbled with the dead bolt, eased the door open, and saw Joseph standing there, rain sluicing down his face.

"We need to talk," he said. "I'm afraid Curtis is out of control."

Timothy McNear

Timothy got out of his car and faced into the wind, feeling the fine droplets on his skin. The storm was abating, blowing inland to the valley and, eventually, to the foothills of the Sierras. The power had come back on, and the bright security spotlights that illuminated the perimeter of the mill shone steadily. Here, well beyond the fence, the spots were dimmer and farther apart, the shadows deeper. But Timothy had no need for light; he'd walked this property more times than he could count.

Love versus hate: that was his relationship with the mill. Love, because it had provided him with a good living and allowed him to prove himself an adept manager, until the lumber business declined so badly that there was no possibility of keeping it operational. Hate, because it had taken his life in a direction he'd never wished it to go.

When he left Cape Perdido for Stanford in the late 1940s, he'd never expected to return. The lumber industry was thriving due to the postwar building boom, but Timothy had no desire to join his father at the helm of the mill. Instead, he would study history, go east for his PhD, and perhaps join the faculty of one of the universities there. Stanford had been a compromise — his parents wanting him close to home — but once he was eligible for a graduate fellowship and able to support himself, the choice of a school would be his own.

He was making his plans to move to New York City, where Columbia had offered the most substantial financial support, when his mother suffered a crippling stroke. Timothy returned to Cape Perdido to help out for the summer, and there he became reacquainted with Caroline Corelli, the daughter of one of the coast's big ranchers, whom he'd known since grade school. Caroline had attended private high school in San Francisco, then studied English literature at Wellesley, and she was not at all happy with her parents' insistence that she return home after taking her bachelor's degree. Over the summer and into the fall, when Timothy put off his move to New York because of his mother's worsening condition, the two discovered they had much in common.

And when Louisa McNear died shortly after the new year, it seemed natural for Caroline and Timothy to marry and move into the big house on the ridge to care for his grieving father. Natural, months later, for Timothy to begin learning the mill's operations. Natural, five years after that, to take over.

*Un*natural, all of it.

Timothy turned and walked toward the main building. The rain had let up entirely now, and brought with it freshness and the scent of kelp. As he walked, he avoided looking toward the pier, where the giant water bag foundered in the surf; he hadn't willingly visited that structure in two decades, and he would not do so tonight.

The doors of the long building, through which two shifts of men had once streamed daily, were secured by a padlock, but Timothy had a key. He fumbled with it, got the lock open, slipped inside. Silence and darkness. He turned on the flashlight he'd brought from the car, went to the switch box, flipped the lever for a set of lights on the equipment track high up toward the ceiling. Then he made his way to the stairs that led to the mezzanine, where the shift supervisor had had his office. Climbed up there and leaned on the railing, looking out over the empty mill floor. He couldn't have articulated why he'd come here tonight or what he was looking for, beyond a desire to reclaim something that had been lost to him.

The building was gutted of its saws and hoists and slings and conveyor belts — sold off at pennies on the dollar at closure — but once it had hummed with activity, the air ringing with the steady whine of the saws. Fifty million board feet of lumber shipped in a good year, a quarter of that in the bad. And the bad had just kept coming. . . .

He'd tried, God knows, but he couldn't keep the mill going. The decision to shut down wasn't one he'd taken lightly, and he hadn't been unfeeling toward his employees' plight. He'd wept the day they sent in the petition asking him to reconsider, but he was tired of a life that had been thrust upon him by circumstance. So he'd pulled the plug, and the workers had left town or, worse, remained, in a state of permanent resentment.

When did everything go so wrong?

Perhaps when Angela died. His little girl, just fourteen, victim of leukemia. Perhaps the first time he'd been unfaithful to Caroline. No excuse for that, or the times that followed, except that he no longer loved his wife. Perhaps the turning point had been much earlier, when they both mistook their common resentment of being trapped in Cape Perdido by familial obligations for a deeper, more lasting connection. It didn't matter, not anymore. He'd made those mistakes and worse, and was left with nothing.

He knew now why he'd come here tonight: to confront what lived inside him and ate at his innards every day.

Is this what your legacy's going to be, old man? Is that what you want them to carve on your tombstone?

He flinched as the thought seemed to echo in his mind.

Legacy: anything handed down from the past. What remains after all else is said and done.

No, he didn't want his final gift to be one of ruin.

I could change that. But it would take a courageous act, and I'm not by nature a courageous man. A courageous man would not have let matters go this far. He would have spoken up, and damn the consequences.

Consequences: the result of what has gone before. Also what remains after all else is said and done.

No, he couldn't accept those particular consequences. He'd long ago plotted out the remainder of his life; it resembled the downside of a bell curve on a graph, allowing for no sudden peaks or valleys.

And yet, there might be a way. . . .

If he thought long and hard, he might find a way. . . .

Sunday, February 22

Jessie Domingo

"I distinctly remember putting the information on Mr. Whitesides's travel arrangements in your packet," Ann, ECC's office manager, said. Her voice had an edge; in spite of her dedication to her job, she probably resented being called at home on a Sunday.

Jessie shifted the receiver slightly and reached for her coffee cup. "I guess I've misplaced them. Will you check on his flight time for me, please?"

"What about Mr. Collier? Did he misplace the information, too?"

"I don't know. He's away from the motel, and I can't reach him." A half-truth; Fitch was across the street at the Blue Moon, having breakfast with the hydrologist.

"All right." Ann sighed. "Let me get to my computer and pull up the file."

Jessie took a sip of weak coffee, then bit into the sugared doughnut that had been one of the offerings on the motel's continental breakfast table. It was stale.

"Here it is," Ann said. "His charter

leaves San Francisco at one o'clock, arrives at two thirty-five."

"When were the travel arrangements made?"

"Last Monday, right after the organization out there accepted our offer of assistance. Someone *will* be at the airport to pick Mr. Whitesides up?"

"Of course."

"Good." Relief was plain in Ann's voice. "And when you see Mr. Collier, will you ask him to check his packet?"

"Yes, I'll do that." Jessie replaced the receiver.

So Eldon Whitesides's trip to Soledad County had been arranged on Monday, before Jessie even received her assignment. She couldn't believe that Ann had neglected to include the information in her trip packet, and contrary to what she'd said on the phone, she knew she hadn't misplaced it. That meant someone had removed it after the file was delivered to her.

Okay, had she been in her cubicle when it arrived? No, that was the day she'd met her mother for lunch near the ABC studios; the file had been on her desk when she returned, and she'd gone over it immediately. During her absence, anyone in the office could have removed the sheet. But who? And more important, why?

To make her think Whitesides's trip was spur-of-the-moment.

Again, why?

A pounding at the door, so hard it rattled in its flimsy frame. Fitch's voice called out, "Ready to go, Jess?"

"Ready." She got up, grabbed her jacket, and joined him at their rental car. A meeting of the Friends and any other interested parties had been called for ten, and for this, apparently, Fitch did not deem her peripheral.

As she slid into the passenger's seat, he said, "Service at that so-called restaurant is slow this morning. Made me late."

"Where's the meeting being held?"

"The Round Barn."

"What's that?"

He started the car and turned it toward the highway. "It belongs to one of the Friends, Lee Longways — you remember him from dinner the other night. He rents it out for dances and other community activities, donated it for this meeting."

"And it's actually round?"

"I suppose so."

"Why, d'you think?"

He frowned at her. "Because it is."

Wasn't he curious about how someone

came to build a barn that was round? Didn't he ever wonder about things like that? Probably not.

She settled in, tugging her seat belt tight as he turned south on the highway. The storm winds had blown the sky clear, and the sea's brilliant blue reflected it. Waves broke against the huge offshore rocks, spewing foam high; on their crests, gulls did takeoffs and landings, drying their wings on the air currents. Jessie spotted a pair of fishing trawlers moving slowly south.

She glanced at Fitch, who hunched over the wheel, gripping it hard with both hands. He oversteered on the first of the switchbacks, then braked sharply to correct. She refrained from distracting him from his driving until they'd descended to the flat stretch by the defunct mill, then asked, "Who's picking up Eldon at the airport?"

"I am."

"Mind if I ride along?"

"No need for that. You'll be more useful here. This meeting is a critical one in terms of assessing the feelings in the community and planning our strategy. I'll brief Eldon on it and go over the legal issues on the drive back from the airport, and meantime you can talk with the people, try to find out things they're not likely to voice in public."

"You mean, if they think there's going to be any more violence. Or if they know who was behind yesterday's shooting."

"Exactly."

"Does anyone know what the Aqueduct people are up to? Do they plan to continue pursuing the project, or what?"

"Aside from talking with the sheriff's department, they've been very quiet. Erickson and his assistant were in the restaurant this morning, reading the out-of-town papers and not saying much of anything, even to each other."

"Maybe I can find out."

"I don't see how that's possible."

"I have my ways."

"Don't do anything foolish, Jess."

She controlled her immediate reaction — which was to snap at him — and after a moment said, "I wouldn't be in this job if I were prone to doing foolish things."

Fitch didn't reply. In a moment he veered across the center line and made a left turn onto a side road that climbed gradually into the hills.

The ridge was rugged along there, the pines thicker than on the slopes above town, intermixed with rough-barked, silvery-leafed trees that exuded a mentholated smell. After a few minutes, the forest gave way to fenced pastureland strewn with outcroppings, where white-faced cattle grazed. Fitch slammed on the brakes as they came up behind an old white pickup truck whose tailpipe spewed a steady stream of exhaust.

"Jesus!" he exclaimed, rolling up his window.

The pickup turned right, through an open gate in the fencing. On a post was taped a crudely lettered sign with an arrow, that said "Friends."

"This is it," Fitch said. "Asshole's polluting the air at a meeting of environmentalists."

"It's an old truck; maybe he can't afford to have it fixed."

"Then he should walk."

"Just don't start anything, okay?"

"Am I the sort of person who starts things?"

Jessie sighed. "Fitch, I barely know you. I don't know what you'll do in a given situation. But my job is to ease the way for you with the community. It strikes me that the best way to get along is to accept these people on their own terms."

He was silent for a moment, dropping

back from the pickup as he carefully navigated the rutted track. "Okay," he finally said, "I'll try to cut them some slack. And I won't start anything. All right?"

"All right."

Ahead of them was a sea of vehicles, parked every which way on a dirt field that was muddy from last night's rain. Beyond them stood the barn. It was painted a boxcar red with black trim; its sides curved, and its peaked roof was topped by a weather vane shaped like a horse. It reminded Jessie of a merry-go-round at the Jersey shore that she'd often ridden as a child. Several people stood outside, talking and smoking, and she could see more through the open doors. Fitch wedged their rental car between two SUVs, and as they crossed toward the barn, Jessie spotted Curtis Hope getting out of the old pickup.

She nudged Fitch. "There's your polluter."

He glanced at Hope and shrugged. "It's a whole other world here."

Inside, the barn was cavernous and noisy, voices echoing off the high beamed ceiling. Around fifty metal folding chairs were set up in the middle of the plank floor, and most were occupied. A platform stood in front of them; from it Joseph and Bernina waved. Jessie and Fitch joined them.

Bernina said, "Joseph's going to call the meeting to order and make a few announcements. Then we want to introduce the two of you. And then, Fitch, could you talk for a while about water law?"

He nodded, and as they sat, Joseph tapped on the microphone he held. The crowd gradually settled down.

"This, folks," Joseph said, "is a continuation of the forum we started at the pier yesterday. Hopefully, nobody'll shoot anything today, because Lee Longways has been good enough to donate us the space, and if his barn or stock get ventilated, he's going to be a mite annoyed."

Polite laughter, but with a nervous edge.

"Speaking of shooting," Joseph went on, "the incident yesterday was regrettable, and the Friends of the Perdido do not condone it in any way. Violence is *never* a good solution to any problem, and we ask that whoever shot that water bag take time to think about his actions and not repeat them. Enough said.

"Now, today we'd hoped to have Gregory Erickson with us again to continue answering your questions, but he's declined to do so, until the question of who destroyed his company's property is cleared up. We are fortunate, however, to have some folks from Environmental Consultants Clearinghouse in New York City, who have agreed to join forces with us in our attempt to persuade the state water resources control board not to grant Aqueduct Systems' application. Jessie Domingo, to my right, is what's known as a community liaison specialist — meaning you can take your ideas or concerns or questions to her directly, and she'll see they're addressed. Feel free to approach her at any time after the formal part of this meeting is over. To my left is Fitch Collier, an attorney specializing in water rights. He's going to explain the legal issues that have bearing on our situation here. Fitch?"

Fitch stood and took the microphone. "Thank you, Joseph. First of all, I have to warn you that water lawyers are the most boring people in the legal community. We're passionate about some of the most intricate and convoluted legislation ever enacted. But we're also passionate about the world's water supply being safeguarded and put to optimal use — and that's what I have in common with all of you. . . ."

Water law, Jessie knew, *was* boring, and

despite his folksy opening, she suspected that Fitch wouldn't hold the crowd's interest for very long. She tuned him out and scanned the faces before her.

Curtis Hope had remained near the barn door, where he leaned against an exposed beam, arms folded across his barrel chest. On Friday night, Hope had held back from the conversation at the restaurant and, in spite of being a board member, had not attended the Friends' meeting at Bernina's. She had not seen him at the pier, either. And in the brief exchange she'd witnessed between him and Joseph, she'd caught an undertone of tension. What was the story on the two of them, anyway?

She shifted her eyes to the right, saw the red-faced heckler, Ike Kudge, standing alone. Today he looked sober and was listening intently to Fitch. When Fitch said, "A complex issue deserves complex consideration, not mere rubber-stamping by a governmental agency," Kudge nodded and muttered, "Right on." Maybe there was more to the man than met the eye.

In the second row of folding chairs, Jessie noticed Steph Pace, who evidently had taken off from her busy restaurant to attend the meeting. Pace was tall and slender, with a cascade of curly chestnut hair; her eyes were almond-shaped, slightly tilted above high cheekbones. A fashion model's face, Jessie thought, except Pace, whom she'd seen wear nothing other than worn jeans and a faded woolen shirt, obviously didn't care about style. She was leaning forward, hands clasped on her knees, but she didn't appear to be watching Fitch. Jessie measured the angle of her gaze, realized that her eyes were fixed on Joseph.

Another relationship she'd like to know more about.

The crowd was growing restless. Fitch was delving into minutiae now — twists and turns of the law that only others of his ilk would find interesting. Jessie tried to signal to him to begin wrapping it up, but her attention was drawn to the door as a pair of sheriff's deputies entered. They stood scanning the crowd, then approached Curtis Hope and spoke briefly with him. He shook his head, spread his hands palms up. One of the deputies spoke again, and Curtis shrugged and followed them outside.

Jessie got to her feet, whispering, "Excuse me," to Joseph, and hurried off the platform. When she came out of the barn, Curtis was standing with the deputies next to a sheriff's department cruiser.

She called, "Curtis, what's happening?" and all three men turned. Curtis looked pale, and the corner of his mouth twitched before he answered.

"I'm wanted at the substation in Calvert's Landing," he said. "A rifle that might've been used on that water bag has turned up. Apparently it's mine."

Joseph Openshaw

"What the hell happened to you?" Joseph said. "I went down to the Landing to spring you from jail, and you were already gone."

"Go away, Joseph." Curtis pushed his beer glass across the bar, signaling to Mark White, the Deluxe's owner, for another round.

"Not this time. Not till I get an explanation why the sheriff's men pulled you out of the meeting."

"Wasn't important. And I wasn't in jail. Even if I had been, I wouldn't've needed you. Jessie Domingo came riding to my rescue, told them they'd better charge me or let me go. For a white woman, she's tough. Must be living in New York City that does it."

"*Jessie* brought you back from the Landing?"

"Right. Guess that's what being a community liaison officer is all about. She asked me a ton of questions on the way back."

"Oh? Like what?"

"About me, you, Steph, Ike Kudge, other people around here." Curtis picked up the fresh beer Mark pushed across the bar, and sipped, looking moody.

"Personal questions, then."

"Yeah. I think she was trying to figure out who's what to whom."

Joseph didn't like that one bit. "You didn't tell her —"

"I didn't tell her much of anything. Just enough to keep her happy and compensate her for getting me out of there. 'Course, there wasn't really any question of them holding me; they just wanted to get the straight story on the rifle."

"What rifle?" Joseph tried to keep his annoyance with Curtis out of his voice. He'd been worried when he learned that his old friend had been taken away from the meeting by the deputies, and he didn't appreciate his cavalier attitude.

"My old thirty-aught-six. They turned it up inside the administration building at the mill. Figure it was used to shoot that water bag. But if they'd checked their own records, they would've saved themselves a lot of trouble. I reported it stolen from my truck almost a year ago. They never did find out who took it."

"Was anything else taken?"

"Some tools. Damn good Porter and Cable drill and bits. Put a crimp in my contracting business till the insurance paid off."

Contracting business, Joseph thought, sure. Curt had been at the top of their high school class, was offered scholarships to three different universities, but instead he'd enlisted in the army. When he returned to Cape Perdido, the service and a broken marriage behind him, he worked construction with the highway department for a few years, then settled into doing repair work only when financial necessity dictated.

Curtis added, "Now that I've answered your questions, will you go away and let me drink in peace?"

Joseph ignored him, thinking how easy it would have been for a sniper to wait on top of the administration building with a gun and choose his opportunity to shoot. But to hide the weapon inside the building and escape without being seen by the deputies who had quickly converged on the scene? Not so easy, unless you knew a quick way to exit, or a secure place within.

"They say where in the building they found the rifle?" he asked Curtis.

"No."

"Or when?"

"I gather they've had it since yesterday but weren't able to trace it to me till this morning. You leaving now?"

"Yeah, I'm leaving." Why waste time in verbal sparring with Curt? Besides, Joseph was due to meet with Bernina, Fitch Collier, Jessie Domingo, and Eldon Whitesides in fifteen minutes.

When he stepped outside, he found the wind had risen, was gusting up the side street from the sea. He faced into it, toward the highway. The sky was still clear, but whitecaps dotted the water; a flock of pelicans skimmed low, looking for their next meal. Joseph glanced at his watch, decided he had time to go home for a heavier jacket. He turned and walked uphill, the wind at his back.

Home was a converted animal shed in Bernina's backyard. At some point, a previous owner had made a square addition to the slope-roofed structure, installed a bathroom and a tiny kitchen; although small and poorly insulated — and on warm days smelling faintly of goat — it perfectly suited Joseph's purposes. He had brought only a few possessions from Sacramento, and those fitted nicely; the rest of his belongings remained in his rental house in Davis, south of the capital, and he suspected that when the lease ran out, he would return to pack them up for storage in Bernina's attic. And then what? He hadn't a clue; he only knew that Sacramento was over for him.

The flashing light on the answering machine indicated he'd had one call. He pressed the play button while reaching for his jacket, heard the voice of Don Huntley, a friend at an environmental organization for which he used to work.

"Joseph, I think you should know that we've had an inquiry about that business last spring. Some guy pretending to be a reporter for the *Bee*. Diane took the call, refused to comment, and it's a good thing, because I checked and nobody at the paper ever heard of him. Sounds like somebody's trying to discredit you, so watch your back."

Joseph replayed the message, listening carefully, then tried to reach Don at home, but got only his machine. In a way, the news didn't surprise him; he'd expected the story would get out one day, had hoped that wouldn't happen until after the situation here was resolved. Maybe on some level he'd hoped it wouldn't surface at all, and that he'd one day be able to return to his life as he'd known it. Well, that was not going to happen, either.

Few people were on the streets as he walked back through town, and there was little traffic on Highway 1. Joseph started across, stopped on the yellow center line, turning first north and then south, contemplating his future here. At times like this, Cape Perdido reminded him of an abandoned movie set. False-fronted buildings, rusted beer signs, dilapidated trucks, sagging power lines — all waiting for the cast and crew to return. But the company had moved on to other, perhaps more exotic locations, leaving this wide spot on the road to be passed by and forgotten.

Joseph shook off the notion and angled across toward the Blue Moon.

Although it was only three-thirty, Steph had agreed to open her restaurant to them as a meeting place. When Joseph stepped inside, he found the bar and adjoining dining room deserted, but from the back came voices. He crossed to the swinging door and pushed through into the kitchen. Steph stood at the chopping-block island, wielding a chef's knife on assorted vegetables, while Arletta O'Neal, her cook, stirred a cast-iron pot on the stove. A television set on top of the doubled-doored stainless steel refrigerator was tuned to a black-and-white movie, but neither woman was watching it.

". . . and if I see one more pale hothouse tomato —" Steph was saying. She broke off, noticing Joseph, and looked at her watch. "That time already?"

He nodded.

"Take over, please," she said to Arletta, pulling her apron off and hanging it on a hook. She led Joseph to the bar area and asked, "Coffee?"

"Please."

Steph poured two cups, and they went to sit at a big round table. "So," she said, "you talk to Curt?"

"Yeah. I finally found him at The Deluxe." He filled her in on what the sheriff's deputies had been after. "You know that detective, Rhoda Swift, don't you?"

"Not well."

"But well enough to call her, ask a few questions?"

"Such as?"

"Where in the administration building they found the rifle. And what they think of Curt's story. If they believe him."

"Why wouldn't they? You said he filed a report of the theft."

"*He* said."

"Why would he lie?"

Joseph shrugged. "I have the feeling Curt's been lying about a number of things lately — or at least telling half-truths."

"Look, we talked about this last night —"

The door opened, and Jessie Domingo and Bernina came in.

"Steph," Joseph said, "will you contact Rhoda Swift? Please?"

She hesitated, then nodded and motioned for the women to join them.

As they got settled at the table, Joseph observed a restrained tension in Jessie's movements. Bernina, clearly in a bad mood, plunked her big tapestry bag down and began rummaging in it, muttering.

"Damn Kleenex, always goes missing at the bottom. God, why do we have to hold this meeting? Couldn't you just handle the man yourself, Joseph? And then send him back where he came from?"

"You have some objection to Mr. Whitesides being here?" Joseph asked.

"Just one more outsider to confuse the issue." Bernina glanced apologetically at Jessie. "You, I don't mind. You seem to relate well to folks here. That lawyer I'm not so sure of, but he probably knows his stuff. But this director of yours — what does he know about a place like this, people like us? Why doesn't he stay in New York, where he belongs?"

Joseph wondered if she would have reacted the same way had Whitesides been a woman, but he knew better than to challenge her on the point. Instead he said mildly, "The meeting won't be all that long, and if you want, you don't have to join us for dinner — although it's an early one, since Mr. Whitesides will want to get checked into his hotel at the Landing."

"That's not the point —"

The door opened, and the subject of the conversation stepped inside. Eldon Whitesides had always been on the heavy side, but prosperity had bulked him up even more. During the nine or ten years since Joseph had last seen him, his once-blond hair and beard had gone totally white, and the skin of his face had been stretched and rounded by his excess poundage. This afternoon his cheeks were ruddy from the cold wind, and he reminded Joseph of a defrocked Santa.

As Joseph rose, Whitesides came toward him, with both hands extended to grasp his. His blue eyes radiated false pleasure as he said, "It's been a long time. You're looking fit, friend."

Perhaps Joseph was not as fit as he

would have liked to be, but he hadn't gained an ounce since their college days. He returned the compliment and quickly disengaged his hands.

"Me? Fit?" Whitesides laughed, patting the stomach that bulged under his suede jacket. "Jessie can testify as to the calories I consume and the exercise I don't get — and she only sees me at the office."

Jessie smiled and shrugged, and Joseph had a quick insight: *she doesn't like him.*

"Where's Fitch?" he asked her.

"He'll be along."

She doesn't like Fitch much, either, but I already knew that.

Joseph introduced Bernina, who growled ungraciously, and Steph, who told them to help themselves to coffee and went back to the kitchen. He wished she would make the call to Rhoda Swift right away, but guessed that was too much to expect when all those vegetables were waiting.

They all sat down again, Whitesides next to Jessie, and Bernina and Joseph opposite them. Seconds later, Fitch came through the door carrying a file. "Man, it's getting cold!" he exclaimed, pulling up a chair. "Glad I stopped back at my room; there was a fax shoved under the door — the report from that private investigator you

hired to check up on Timothy McNear."
He nodded at Whitesides.

From the startled expression on Jessie's face and the way she stiffened, Joseph assumed this was the first she'd heard about an investigator.

Bernina frowned and leaned forward. "Why were you checking up on him?" she asked Whitesides.

"We thought if he could be persuaded not to let Aqueduct trench and lay pipe across his property, our problem would go away."

"And for that you had to hire a private investigator?"

Uh-oh, Joseph thought, never should've brought these two together.

"Yes," Whitesides said patiently. "In order to persuade someone, you need to know who you're dealing with."

Bernina frowned more deeply.

Before she could comment, Joseph said, "I could have given you background on McNear. I've known the man my whole life."

Whitesides made a motion of dismissal. "Not deep background, however."

"You mean the dirt."

"You always did tell it like it is, Joseph. Yes, the dirt. When it comes to the persuasion game, everyone has his weak point. Have we found McNear's, Fitch?"

"Unfortunately, no."

Joseph glanced at Bernina; now her lips were pursed, her eyes thoughtful.

Fitch opened his file. "Our investigator went all the way back to the beginning, per my request. Timothy was born in nineteen-thirty to Warner and Louisa McNear, an only child. Father was the second owner of the mill, bought it from the Breyer brothers in nineteen-seventeen, and turned control over to Timothy five years after he graduated from Stanford. While at Stanford, his academic record was excellent, and his student deferment — plus his father's influence with a highly placed politico — kept him out of Korea. Married Caroline Corelli, of the Corelli ranching family, eight months after he graduated. By all accounts it was not a particularly good marriage, and McNear was rumored to have had two long-running affairs, but both women and the wife are dead now, so there's no leverage there. The couple had one son, Robert, and a daughter, Angela, who died in her teens. McNear is said to have been a good employer and run the mill well; he tried to find a buyer before he closed it down, but with no success. By then he'd been widowed sixteen years. The son was also widowed, had two boys, Maxwell and Shelby, and lived with McNear for a year after his wife died. Was a graphic artist and had no interest in taking over at the mill, moved to Australia in nineteen-eighty-four. Some estrangement there, according to the housekeeper, who's been with McNear for over twenty years. She's not sure —"

Joseph interrupted the recitation. "Your investigator was snooping around here, talking with people who know McNear?"

Fitch looked irritated at the interruption. "That's what investigators do, Joseph. Anyway, the housekeeper doesn't know the details of the estrangement, but she says McNear has lived a fairly reclusive life since his son left. He's a drinker, but regulates it. No other known vices at present. I'm afraid there's nothing we can use."

Beside Joseph, Bernina cleared her throat. "Do you often use methods like this, Mr. Whitesides?" Her tone was more interested than critical.

"When the situation is serious enough to warrant it."

Jessie said, "Excuse me, Eldon, but it was my understanding that you were planning to approach this situation on the legal issues. Set a precedent so what's happening here couldn't happen elsewhere. That being the case, why are you trying to cut short the process by getting leverage on McNear?"

"Because, my dear, we need a fallback position in case the state board rules against us."

"He's right, Jessie," Bernina said. "Points of law don't always impress these bureaucrats."

"I can't believe you approve of these methods!"

"Sometimes you have to get down and dirty." Bernina actually smiled at Whitesides.

Joseph had been afraid the two would lock horns, but he wasn't sure he liked this sudden rapprochement, either.

Jessie ignored Bernina, said to Eldon, "All right, if there had been any dirt in that file, would you use it? Right away? Before the board meets?"

"Yes, Jessie, we would use it, because there isn't time to handle the situation as we'd planned. Violence has been committed here, and no matter how the Friends decry it, if it escalates, the press and public are bound to blame them. Our job now is to forestall further violence that

156

will make all environmental organizations look bad."

Typical Eldon Whitesides bullshit, Joseph thought. *I'd like to know what he's really up to.*

"Well," Jessie said, "since there's no dirt, what do you propose we do?"

Whitesides grinned, a malevolent Santa now. "Perhaps," he said, "we'll have to manufacture some."

In the shocked silence that followed, he winked and said, "Just joking."

Sure you are, Eldon. Sure.

Steph Pace

Steph seldom left the Blue Moon during the three daily meal services, so missing two today would be something of a record. But at this time of year, Sundays were slow, and she was sure her employees could handle dinner as well as they'd handled lunch and the tail end of breakfast. As she set out for the meeting she'd arranged with Rhoda Swift, she felt a sense of freedom and again wondered if she ought to move away from Cape Perdido and get into a new line of work.

She'd fallen into the restaurant business more or less by accident. When she moved to Oregon after high school, she'd quickly realized how ill prepared she was for any kind of job other than the waitressing she'd done during the summers. Five years of working in the food service industry in the Portland area had taught her a great deal, and when she returned to Cape Perdido, the then owner of the Blue Moon — a good cook but a poor businessman — hired her as his manager. When he decided

158

to retire, Steph's mother offered to loan her the money to buy him out. And eleven years later, here she was, as sick of the daily grind as her former employer had been.

Trouble was, while marginally profitable, the Blue Moon's remote location and highly seasonal trade would not make it an easy sell. And even if she were able to find a buyer, what would she do then? The restaurant business was all she knew. She supposed she could start over in whatever new location she chose, but that would defeat the purpose. No, she'd probably be at the Blue Moon, contending with the winter shortage of interesting vegetables, till the day she died.

The lights of Calvert's Landing appeared before her, strung out on a crescent along the shore. She'd decided the best way to approach Rhoda Swift was in person. When she called to ask for a meeting, the detective had sounded surprised, and then suggested dinner at a restaurant at the town pier. "You can check out the competition," she told her.

Steph didn't take the comment seriously; there was no competition between her place and Tai Haruru. The seafood restaurant was tourist oriented, served food that greatly eclipsed Arletta's plain cooking, and offered live entertainment on the weekends. Even on this quiet Sunday night, the parking lot was crowded. Steph left her car near the base of the pier and walked past the boarded-up processing shed that was the last remnant of the Landing's once-robust days as a fishing port. Inside the restaurant, which occupied the entire top floor of the pier's long wooden commercial building, people bellied up two deep to the ornate carved bar that in the thirties had been hauled north by wagon from a former San Francisco speakeasy. Steph went to the hostess station and was shown to Swift's booth, in the rear section under a huge stuffed swordfish.

Rhoda greeted her warmly, as if they were good friends rather than acquaintances. After they'd ordered wine and consulted the menus, Steph apologized for taking up her time on a Sunday.

"Think nothing of it," Rhoda said. "I've been at the substation all day, and you've given me a chance to relax and unwind before I go home. Besides, my man's in New York till April, so I had nothing planned for tonight, other than tackling a sink-full of dirty dishes."

Steph had heard that Rhoda was involved

with a prominent East Coast journalist, Guy Newberry, who owned a vacation home south of the Landing, near Deer Harbor. "He lives back there in the wintertime?" she asked.

"Right. Says he can't take the rain here. And when I visit him there, I can't take the snow. But we've worked out a pretty good part-time arrangement."

The waitress came to take their orders — shrimp scampi, the best on the Soledad Coast — and after she departed, Rhoda said, "I assume you wanted this meeting because of the situation up your way. You have something to tell me?"

"Actually, I'm after information. I understand you brought Curtis Hope in for questioning today. He's a friend of mine, and I'm concerned."

Rhoda broke off a piece of sourdough from the loaf in the basket and buttered it, eyeing Steph thoughtfully. "Have you spoken with your friend?"

"No. Apparently he's holed up in a bar, and that bothers me, too."

"I see. Well, his drinking may be cause for concern, but our interest in him isn't anything to worry about. It seems a rifle that he reported stolen last year was used to shoot that water bag."

So Curt wasn't lying.

"Are you sure it's the right weapon?"

"Yes. We were able to recover one of the spent bullets from the bag — which, by the way, is still wallowing off the pier at the mill — and it's a match."

"And where did you find the rifle?"

"In the admin building. There's a row of lockers where the clerical workers hung their coats, and it was at the back of one of them, behind some old overalls."

"So the shooter climbed down from the roof, went inside, and hid the rifle before your deputies got there?"

"That's right. They didn't search inside until later — we had only a few officers there, and given the panic, their first priority was crowd control. The shooter probably waited in the building, then took advantage of the confusion to slip away."

"Wouldn't he have to know the building well, in order to find a hiding place and get away in time?"

"We're assuming he — or she — checked it out beforehand and made a plan. The mill site isn't all that secure."

So it wasn't a spur-of-the-moment shooting. How far ahead was it planned? As long as a year, when Curt reported the rifle missing?

162

My God, what am I thinking? A year ago we didn't know any of this was going to happen. Besides, Curt isn't a violent man . . . is he?

"Steph?" Rhoda said. "You okay?"

"Oh." She looked down distractedly at the glass of wine the waitress was setting in front of her. "Just worried about the situation."

Rhoda nodded. "Understandable, since you and Joseph and Curtis used to hang together in high school. Somebody else was part of your group, right? Mack Kudge?"

Now, why does she have to remember that? Probably because younger kids always notice what the older kids are doing.

"Right."

"We still have an open file on his murder, you know. Back-burnered, of course."

"I guess it'll always be a mystery, what happened to him."

"You never know. Every so often something turns up unexpectedly and there's a break in one of these old cases."

"Like that mass murder down at Point Deception a while back?"

Rhoda nodded. "Thirteen years we waited for our break."

"But Mack — that was even longer ago, twenty years."

"Thirteen, twenty — not all that much difference, once the case is cold. It's probably coincidental that Mack's body was found on the pier at the mill, but it still makes you wonder."

"Well, he worked there."

"Wasn't shot there, though. The body had been moved from someplace else."

"So what're you saying? That there could be a connection to what's going on now? That seems awfully far-fetched to me."

"I'm not saying anything except what I said before — you never know what might turn up." Rhoda paused as the waitress set their plates in front of them." Then she smiled at Steph and added, "Bon appetit."

Timothy McNear

He'd thought on the problem all day, and his head throbbed from the effort. A throbbing that hadn't been helped by too many generous helpings of Scotch. Now it was well on toward midnight, and if he didn't take himself downstairs and eat some of the roast that was drying out in the oven, he'd have a monumental hangover in the morning.

But he remained in his chair in the dark loft, still trying to solve the seemingly unsolvable.

There has to be a way to turn this thing around without paying the ultimate price. Has to be a way to take the weapon that's aimed at me and aim it back at them.

The main difficulty, of course, was that he had allowed his fear and rage to get in the way of rational thinking. He'd replayed his initial meeting with the CEO of Aqueduct Systems again and again, relived his disbelief and shock and horror. It seemed now as if he'd capitulated much too easily. And last night, when Gregory Erickson had shown up unannounced but not unexpected, to warn

165

him not to change his mind . . .

What happened to the man who was once such a hard negotiator? When did I become this shrinking, cringing creature?

Erickson had presented no proof at any time, but he didn't need to show documents or name sources to convince Timothy. What the man knew could have come only from one of three people. Three people who, Timothy had thought, had good reason never to reveal their knowledge to anyone.

He reached for the decanter with a shaking hand and poured more Scotch. So what if he had a hangover tomorrow? Or the day after, or the day after that? His mind, once keenly analytical, had failed him, allowed his emotions to rule it. He was no better than a child shivering in the dark. If this was what the rest of his life was to be, he couldn't face it sober.

Timothy drank and stared at the window. From the southwest came a reddish glow. At first he thought he was imagining it, but it grew brighter, more intense.

Fire!

He leaned forward, peering, then got up and went to stand by the glass. His heart beat erratically as the flames reached from behind and below the downslope and lit up the midnight sky.

The mill — my God, it's the mill!

He dropped the glass he still held, gripped the window frame for support. Downstairs the phone was ringing, but he ignored it. The shriek of sirens rose from the highway — fire trucks heading south from the volunteer station. The phone stopped ringing, then immediately started again.

Timothy remained by the window, watching his past go up in flames.

Monday,
February 23

Jessie Domingo

Jessie was on the phone talking with her roommate, Erin Sullivan, when she heard the sirens. It was two minutes after three in New York, and Erin had called, half smashed, with a story about meeting Jessie's ex-boyfriend, Matt Westley, in one of the clubs they frequented. The story involved Matt and his date getting into a fight and being forcibly ejected, and it depressed Jessie because it reminded her of her poor judgment when it came to men. She was, she'd come to realize, a practical, intelligent woman with an impractical, unintelligent attraction to bad boys, which no amount of self-awareness had so far been able to cure.

In New York she wouldn't have paid the sirens any attention, but here they gave her a convenient excuse to cut the conversation short.

"Something's happening," she said to Erin. "Got to go." And quickly placed the receiver in its cradle.

As she stepped outside her motel room, a fire truck streaked by, its lights flashing; a

171

highway patrol car followed. She hurried across the lot and peered after them. To the south the sky glowed red.

Jessie ran back to the motel and pounded on Fitch's door. He opened it wearing a bathrobe, his hair matted down on one side. Fumbling his glasses on, he said, "What?"

"Didn't you hear the sirens?"

"Yeah. So?"

"There's a big fire south of here."

"So?"

"Think, Fitch — what's to the south?"

"The . . . my God, the mill!"

"Throw some clothes on and let's go see."

"Half a minute." He closed the door.

Jessie grabbed a jacket from her room, hurried to their rental car, and had it started and turned around by the time Fitch came outside. Before he could get his seat belt latched, she gunned it out onto the highway. Fitch gripped the dashboard, leaning forward and staring at the red sky.

"Jesus," he said, "the whole mill must be burning."

"And what do you bet it's arson?"

"Don't get ahead of yourself."

"Fitch? Hello? That mill's been shut down, unguarded, for five years, and it accidentally catches on fire now? The day after someone sabotaged that water bag?"

Fitch didn't reply. When Jessie glanced over at him, she saw he was gnawing on his lower lip; in the light from the dash, he looked very pale.

"What?" she asked.

"Don't drive so fast."

Jessie accelerated into the first of the switchbacks.

"Come on, there's no reason —"

Red lights flashed behind them, reflecting off the chiseled slope to their left. Jessie yanked the wheel, and the car skidded onto the shoulder above the cliff, spewing gravel. As she got the skid under control, an ambulance rushed by, siren wailing.

"Christ!" Fitch exclaimed. "You almost hit the guardrail!"

She closed her eyes, gripped the wheel with slick fingers, her foot trembling on the brake. "Sorry," she said. "I'll be more careful."

"See that you are." Fitch's voice shook; it was more of a plea than an order.

Jessie steered back onto the highway and drove more slowly into the next switchback. When they came out on its far side, she could see that fire engulfed most of the buildings on the point; it shimmered and leaped skyward, sending up great clouds of smoke and sparks that the light wind caught and blew inland.

"My God," Fitch said. "If they don't contain it quickly, it'll spread to the ridge. All that timber . . ."

Grimly she sped through the last switchback, straightened the car out on the flatland. Ahead she saw flashing red and blue lights and two highway patrol cars positioned at right angles across the pavement. A logging truck and three cars were lined up in front of them, and beyond them emergency vehicles moved.

Jessie pulled onto the shoulder and got out of the car, not waiting for Fitch. The air was warm and thick with smoke, the flashing lights disorienting. She spotted a knot of people near the patrol cars and moved toward them.

". . . never get this load to San Jose by morning if I've gotta detour along the ridge road," a bearded man was saying.

"What is it?" a woman asked. "Some kind of factory?"

Jessie skirted them, kept going toward a patrolman who stood in front of the cars. A fire truck was scaling the slope on the eastern side of the highway — a preventive measure, in case the flames jumped the pavement. The patrolman held up his hand.

"Please step back, ma'am."

"Can you tell me —"

"Please, ma'am, get back in your vehicle."

She turned, bumped into Fitch. His mouth was slack, and the dancing firelight reflected off the lenses of his glasses. From behind her came a sound like a subway train roaring into a station. She whirled in time to see the roof of one of the long buildings collapse, a fireball blossoming above it.

"It can't be," Fitch said, his voice close to a sob. "It can't!" He stared at the flames, running his tongue over dry lips.

Jessie grasped his arm. "Fitch? What can't be?"

"You don't want to know, Jess. Believe me, you don't."

He started toward their car, but Jessie went after him.

"You think Eldon hired someone to set this fire, don't you? Had evidence planted that will incriminate Timothy McNear? He claimed his comment about manufacturing dirt was a joke, but I wouldn't put it past him!"

"Leave it, Jess." Fitch faced her. In the glow of the flames his face was drawn and pasty. "I shouldn't've said anything."

"Well, you did, so out with the rest of it."

"Not till I speak with Eldon."

"We'll both speak with him. Tonight."

Fitch just stood there, arms limp at his sides. After a moment he shook himself, as if awakening from a bad dream. "Okay," he said slowly, "but we should talk in person, and I don't know how we're going to manage that when he's staying down at Calvert's Landing."

"Why . . . ?" Jessie glanced back at the line of waiting vehicles. "Oh, right, the road's blocked." She spotted the bearded man standing by his logging rig and hurried up to him. "You said something earlier about a detour along the ridge. Where is that?"

"Make a U-turn and take Adams Grade Road — it's about half a mile up; you'll see a bunch of mailboxes at its foot. It dead-ends at Crestline, and you follow that south, cut back to the coast highway on Angels Gulch, just above Calvert's Landing. But I gotta warn you: those roads're narrow and badly paved. You'd be better off waiting till this mess is cleared up."

"Thanks!" Jessie ran back to Fitch. "There's a detour. Let's go."

Anything, even a narrow, badly paved road, was preferable to waiting.

Joseph Openshaw

Joseph watched as the highway patrolman urged the New Yorkers back toward the waiting line of vehicles, then slipped around the cruisers and stepped over the sawhorse barricade that had been hastily assembled behind them. A truck from the Cape Perdido Volunteer Fire Department — antiquated, like all the emergency vehicles in this poor county — lumbered by. Smoke clogged his nostrils, and when he breathed through his mouth, he coughed. The wind from the west felt superheated and carried with it the shouts of men and thrum of pumps and crackling of flames.

An ambulance stood on the pavement some twenty yards away; a paramedic had set up a table next to it to dispense bottled water to firemen. Joseph veered over there, peered inside the ambulance. Dave Crespo, a lanky redhead who had played basketball with Joseph in high school, was taking the vital signs of a firefighter in a heavy blue-and-yellow suit. The man's face was smudged and sweat-slicked, his eyes tearing. Crespo removed the blood-pressure cuff and said, "I think you ought to sit it out for a while, guy."

"No can do." The firefighter thrust his arm back into his sleeve and zipped his suit, clapped Dave on the shoulder, and climbed down from the ambulance. On his way past the table he snagged a bottle of water.

Crespo spotted Joseph, shook his head. "I tell them to take it easy, but they don't listen. I never listened when I was a volunteer, either."

"Any injuries?" Joseph asked.

"Not so far."

"CDF here?"

"Not yet. They're coming up from Signal Port and Westhaven. If they get here soon and this wind doesn't pick up, maybe they can contain it before it jumps to timber." The California Department of Forestry's fire department had the edge on the volunteers: state financed, it was well equipped and staffed by full-time professionals.

"They'd better hurry. Our guys need all the help they can get." The volunteers Joseph had seen were tiring fast, but like the man who hadn't heeded Dave's advice, they wouldn't rest. Fire was the single largest threat to life and safety in the county; the volunteers would fight it till the last ember was extinguished. "Any idea when this started?"

"Call came in around eleven forty, from a passing motorist with a cellular. Was going pretty strong by the time our people got here."

"Any idea of the cause?"

Crespo shook his head.

"You think this could have been arson?"

"Wouldn't surprise me. The buildings are old and dry. A little accelerant poured in the right places . . ." He shrugged.

"Spread fast, didn't it?"

"Yeah, it did. Makes you wonder." A pair of firefighters approached, one man leaning heavily on the other, arm around his shoulders, soot-blackened face contorted in pain. Crespo went to meet them.

Joseph crossed the highway to the chain-link fence surrounding the mill site. It was hot to the touch, and on the slope behind it, men were digging a trench. Beyond them, a yellow-orange pyre burned furiously. On one of the buildings to the north, flames rushed along the roof in a crazy zigzag pattern and shot up the tall smoke-stack, sparks whirling against the sky. For a short time the stack was a brilliant tower of light; then it shuddered and began to crumble. Joseph thought it cried out, realized it was his own voice he heard, filled with a grief that threatened to choke him. A part of the past was dying, a part of him along with it.

Sirens sounded behind him — two CDF trucks moving swiftly up the highway from the south. A cheer rose up from the men trenching behind the fence as the trucks sped through the gate by the guardhouse.

Joseph turned away. A man could stand only so much ruin. As he moved back toward the paramedics, intending to volunteer his services, he caught sight of somebody standing on the other side of the barricade. A man whom he couldn't see clearly, a man who spotted him at the same time, whirled, and fled.

Joseph followed.

Steph Pace

Steph stood on the front porch of her clapboard cottage, bathrobe wrapped tightly around her, and watched the conflagration. The house was east of town, on a rise that had been logged off decades ago, and the fire consuming the mill was visible above the roofs of its neighbors. She could hear excited voices — other people on their porches — and see a knot of people in the middle of the street, but she made no move to join them. To her it was not an exciting occasion, or one for sharing.

She had no doubt the mill would be a total loss. Even if it had been daylight and they'd been able to send out the tanker planes, it would have done little good. The best she could hope for was that no one got killed or injured, and that the flames did not jump the highway into the timberland.

She laughed — a mirthless, dry sound that hurt her throat. What a way for Timothy McNear to have his defunct mill razed! She wouldn't be surprised if he'd hired an arsonist to do the job.

I know what the old bastard's doing.

Standing in that loft of his and watching. But what is he feeling? Does he feel? Once I would have said yes, but now I don't know.

The phone rang, and Steph went inside to answer it. Her mother, calling from Westhaven, the southernmost town in the county.

"Can you see the fire, Steffi? Is it the mill?"

"Yes, Mom."

"Can they save any of it?"

"No, I don't think so."

"It's God's retribution. You know it is."

Steph felt her way through the dark room to the sofa, curled up there, and pulled an afghan over her bare feet. "I suppose so."

"That man. That evil, evil man."

"Mom . . ."

"You know what he did to Alice. She never would've died the way she did —"

"Ancient history."

"Ancient history to you, maybe. But she was my best friend, and she killed herself because of him."

"Mom, can we do this another time?"

"What have you got going at two in the morning that's so important? Oh!" Her mother's voice became sly. "Somebody's with you. Joseph? Is Joseph there?"

"Joseph is *not* here. He never comes here. That was all over years ago."

"Nonsense. I know he spends time at the restaurant every afternoon, and I know he was at your house last night. Stayed till all hours."

"How did you — ?"

"I have my sources."

"Dorothy Crane. She's always looking out her window —"

"Is it her fault he showed up just when the blackout ended?"

"Mom, it wasn't . . ."

"Yes?"

"Nothing. I have to go now."

"Steffi, I've always thought you and Joseph would get back together. Don't spoil it this time."

"Good night, Mom."

Steph went back outside. The glow wasn't as intense now, and there was no sign that the blaze had spread to the ridge. Still, she remained on her porch long after the neighbors had returned to their homes and beds. The phone rang twice, but fearing further inquisition from her mother, she let the machine pick up. Yes, it was Mom, sounding mighty irritated.

I've always thought you and Joseph would get back together. Don't spoil it this time.

I didn't spoil it the last time, Mom, and neither did he. You'd be surprised if I told you what did.

Timothy McNear

The southwest sky still glowed red, but a call from the county fire marshal had assured him that, while the mill was a total loss, there was no longer danger of the flames spreading into a catastrophic forest fire. Tomorrow he would drive down to the point, meet with officials, and view the ruins. There would be an investigation, and insurance claims to file. But now he sat at his kitchen table, drinking coffee that was not really necessary because shock and rage had sobered him, perhaps for all time.

The mill had stood on its jut of land since 1862, its natural harbor making it easily accessible for the schooners that plied the coast. There had been boom times when the supply of redwood seemed as inexhaustible as the demand; bust times when its owners had regretted the lack of foresight that had depleted the timber, and the unstable economy that further conspired against them. But over the years, the mill had been a constant fixture of the Cape, its life's blood. Even after he'd been forced to close it down, it had stood as a monument to the past. And now it was gone.

Gone, because of one man's greed and determination to have his way no matter what the cost. He had no doubt the fire had been set on orders from Gregory Erickson.

Is this what your legacy's going to be, old man? A heap of ashes and twisted metal? A river where nothing lives?

No, it isn't. And damn the consequences.

The worm has turned.

Jessie Domingo

The Tides Inn, where Eldon Whitesides was staying, sat on a bluff above the Calvert's Landing municipal pier. Its white clapboard facade was brightly lighted even after three in the morning, the floods' beams silvering the leaves of the tall trees — eucalyptus, she'd been told they were called — that grew around it. Jessie followed a steep driveway that led from the parking lot of the long, dark-wood commercial building at the foot of the pier to the inn's reception area. The lobby was also brightly lit, and she spotted a young Latino man nodding off behind the desk.

Fitch said, "Eldon's in room two-ten." His voice was strained. He'd said little on the harrowing ride along the dark and winding ridge road, except to caution her repeatedly to hold her speed down.

She scanned a sign that pointed the way to the various units, then drove to the end of a wing that extended far out onto the bluff. Two-ten would be upstairs, with a balcony that faced the sea — no modest lodgings for the boss, though Fitch and Jessie were crammed into tiny rooms that smelled of Lysol.

She started to get out of the car, but Fitch put a hand on her arm. "Jess, let's not do this now. I've been thinking we should wait till morning, when we're both more clearheaded."

She shook his hand off. "And do what instead — sleep in the car?"

"That's not such a bad idea. I'm exhausted, and you must be, too."

"I couldn't sleep anyway, not knowing what you suspect."

"I may be wrong. At least let me explain to Eldon why we've come. Don't go blustering in there making accusations."

"All right, let's go."

As they crossed the parking area, Jessie could hear the boom of the surf on the rocks below; the scent of the trees that crowded in beside the building was sharp and their leaves whispered in the light breeze. The units were dark, except for one at the far end whose white curtains were backlit, and when she and Fitch climbed the outside staircase and reached its door, she saw it was Whitesides's. She knocked, and they waited.

No response.

"Maybe he's sleeping," Fitch whispered. He looked as if he would welcome any excuse to go back downstairs to the car.

"With the lights on?" Jessie knocked harder.

"Jesus, you'll wake up the entire place!"

She ignored him, went to the window, and tried to peer around the curtains. All she saw was the end of a beige sofa. She went back to the door, rattled the handle. It turned, and the door swung open into a beige and brown room that was far larger and more attractive than her own at the Shorebird; the walls were adorned with seascapes, and a king-size bed stood in an alcove. The bed was empty, its comforter slightly rumpled; a suitcase sat open on a rack, and a laptop and briefcase rested on a glass-topped table by the window overlooking the balcony. Jessie glanced around; the bathroom door was open, the light off.

"So where is he?" Her voice sounded unnaturally loud; behind her, Fitch seemed to have stopped breathing.

She crossed to the bathroom, flicked on the light. A shaving kit sat on the vanity, and a couple of towels were crumpled on the floor.

"He must be around someplace," Fitch said. "Maybe he went out."

"Where? Nothing's open; this town rolled up the sidewalks hours ago. Besides, you drove him here after dinner; he doesn't have a car."

"He could've gone to get ice or for a walk —"

"I don't think so. We passed the ice machine on the way in. And that bluff doesn't look like the kind of place you'd want to wander around in the dark."

Fitch spread his hands. "Then I can't imagine what's happened to him."

Jessie went to the bureau, examined the objects arrayed there. Watch. Spare change. Wallet. She slipped it open. Eldon's, all right. His face smiled up from his New York driver's license as if he'd just told a clever joke and was terribly pleased with himself.

"Jess?" Fitch said. "What the hell happened here?"

She crossed to the table where the laptop sat. It was in sleep mode; when she restarted it, she saw that Whitesides had been using his e-mail. On the computer's screen was a half-written reply to Tom@LBT.com. She scanned it, said, "Fitch, what's the name of the investigator you were using?"

"Tom Little, at LBT Investigations in San Francisco."

"Take a look at this. It's dated yesterday, around the time Eldon was in the meeting with us."

Fitch came over and read aloud, " 'Mr. Whitesides — The materials on Gregory Erickson and Neil Woodsman are on their way to you by special messenger. Do you want me to continue gathering information on Joseph Openshaw? TL.' And at nine that evening Eldon replied, 'I'm looking forward to receiving the documents. Please proceed on Openshaw. Note that the billing for this job should be sent to my home address. I'd like confirmation of the rumors you reported ASAP and . . .' I understand why he's having Erickson and Woodsman investigated, but why Joseph?"

"Exactly. Why is he investigating somebody who's supposed to be on our side?"

Joseph Openshaw

Joseph stood in the shelter of the trees, watching the shack in the clearing. It was up a steep, mud-slick trail from the reservation road, next to a little creek that flowed freely now but in months would be nothing more than a trickle. Pines and tanbark oak encroached on the leaning corrugated-iron structure, and light — probably from an oil lamp — seeped around its poorly fitting door. Joseph had been waiting close to an hour — for what, he wasn't sure.

The shack had been there as long as he could remember — a relic from the days when the bark of the oaks had been stripped and hauled by wagon to Signal Port, for shipment south to hide-tanning factories. In their youth, he and his friends had used the shack as a refuge from often drunken and abusive parents, smoked their first cigarettes and drunk their first beers there, and later had had their first women within its dark confines. Now there were no more young people on the rez, merely a handful of elders and middle-aged folk like

Curtis, and the shack stood abandoned. Or so Joseph had thought until he'd followed Harold Kosovich there tonight.

He had recognized the odd little man after he fled the scene of the fire and climbed into an old blue Buick parked by the roadside. By the time Joseph retrieved his van and caught up with the car, it had passed through Cape Perdido and was turning into the hills toward the rez. Even though there were no other vehicles on the road, Harold didn't appear to know he was being followed. He ditched the car at the boarded-up community center and took the trail into the woods. Joseph parked and went after him.

The night was cold here on the ridge, and the breeze brought with it the stench of the fire. Joseph tucked his hands into his pockets, gazed up through the trees at a star-shot, smoke-streaked sky. Even the night birds were silent, sensing danger.

After a while Joseph felt a stir of alarm. It was too quiet in the clearing, and the lamplight burned steadily in the shack, showing no motion. What was Kosovich doing in there? And why had he run when he saw Joseph at the mill?

He moved slowly from the trees' shelter, the tall grass whispering around his legs, twigs and pinecones snapping under his feet. There was no sound from the shack's occupant as he put his eye to the crack around the door and peered inside.

The lamp sat on the rotting board floor, its glow washing over the rusted walls and ceiling. Several cardboard cartons were stacked to one side, and empty liquor bottles lay everywhere. In the far corner was what looked like a pile of rags.

Not rags — a bed. Harold's been living here. What happened to his trailer?

Joseph entered and moved closer to the makeshift bed, the hairs on the back of his neck prickling. He smelled alcohol and something else that he couldn't identify before he saw the bottle of cheap whiskey lying on its side, liquid puddling around an empty prescription vial. Kneeling, he pulled away a tattered gray blanket and stared into Harold's still face.

Overdosed. While I stood outside, doing nothing.

He grabbed the little man's arm, undid the cuff button of his denim shirt, felt for a pulse. Couldn't find one. He pressed his fingers against Harold's neck, thought he detected a fluttering.

He reached into his pocket for his cell phone, realized he'd left it on the seat in the van. Damn thing was never where it should be, but most likely the emergency lines would be jammed because of the fire. He hesitated, then pulled Harold from his ragged nest, and hoisted him over his shoulder. The little man was no more burden than a sack of flour. As Joseph moved toward the door, his eyes rested on the oil lamp; there had been enough destruction tonight; he couldn't risk it setting a fire here on the ridge.

Grunting, he bent to extinguish it. Then he straightened, carried Harold outside and down the slippery path toward the home of the one person he knew up here who could help.

Steph Pace

When the phone began ringing at six, Steph answered it, determined to blast her mother's eardrum for calling so early. But the voice that greeted her, while familiar, was one she'd never expected to hear.

"Miss Stephanie," Timothy McNear said, "I wish to meet with you. Today, if at all possible."

His commanding tone was as she remembered it: so self-assured it didn't allow for protest or refusal. When she'd worked as nanny to his grandsons, he'd addressed her in the same way, whether the matter at hand was trivial ("Make sure those toys are picked up, please") or important ("Never forget to fasten the boys' seat belts when you're driving them"). He had intimidated her then, and he frightened her now.

When she didn't speak, he added, "I know you have no reason to agree to see me, and I wouldn't ask if it weren't important."

She cleared her throat. "Can you give me some idea of why — ?"

"I'm sure you know."

The words put a chill on her, and all she could say was, "When?"

"Anytime, and I'll come to you. You name the place, but it should be a private one."

A private place could be dangerous.

"I'll have to think about this and get back to you."

"That's fine. I understand fully. But you're not to mention this call to anyone. Is that clear?"

"Perfectly."

"I have a meeting with the fire marshal and the sheriff's people down at the mill this morning, but you can leave a message here on my machine. The number is the same; I'm sure you remember it."

He hung up, but Steph stood with the receiver pressed to her ear until the dial tone began. Finally she replaced it in its cradle and pulled her robe more closely around her — a futile gesture, since the chill that gripped her body came from within.

What to do? Call Joseph? Or Curtis? No, McNear had said to tell no one, and she was afraid to disobey him.

Alone — that was how she'd have to face McNear. And maybe that wasn't so bad. Maybe then, for her at least, the long nightmare would finally be over.

Timothy McNear

There. It was done. He had made the call, broken the long silence. Now it was up to her.

Timothy contemplated the telephone, taking a grim pleasure in his new resolve.

Stephanie Pace, he knew, had grown into a strong woman, a far cry from the lovely but timid high school girl who had come into his home and lived in his servants' quarters, to care for Max and Shelby. Over the intervening years he'd watched her from a distance. Surrounded by employees and the members of the charitable organizations she volunteered for, she nevertheless gave the impression of being a loner. Although she was reputed to be an excellent businesswoman and a reliable member of the community, he sensed something unpredictable and wild in her, firmly held in check but capable of bursting forth, given the right provocation. Just what gave him that impression, he couldn't say, but for some time now he'd been waiting for her to do the unexpected.

Just so long as it wasn't today.

And if she did? If she refused to meet with him and tell him what he needed to know?

Then he'd go after her, verbally break her down. He'd intimidated her in the past, and he'd intimidated her on the phone just now. There was no way she could resist the kind of pressure he'd bring to bear.

An eyewitness.

One of only three people. And Stephanie Pace would know which. Once she gave him a name, the way to proceed would come clear, no question about that. And then he would face the consequences.

The hell with the consequences, old man. The hell with them.

Jessie Domingo

"I think we should call the sheriff," Fitch said.

It was nearly nine, and they were seated in a coffee shop on the highway in Calvert's Landing. They'd waited in Eldon Whitesides's motel room until seven, hoping he'd return, and then made discreet inquiries to the staff and the town's one taxi company. No one had seen him since he'd checked in, and no cab had picked him up. They'd then driven around looking for possible places he might be, and even walked the bluff trail near the Tides Inn, Jessie's overactive imagination conjuring up images of his body lying at the cliff's bottom or floating in the sea. Eldon, apparently, had vanished without a trace.

Jessie said, "Even if we reported him missing, they probably have the same waiting period as we do at home and wouldn't do anything about it yet. And besides, if what we suspect about the fire at the mill is true . . . well, we've got the foundation's reputation to think about."

"You're right."

Fitch's eyelids drooped as he leaned on his elbow and stared out the window at the traffic on the highway. Jessie was sure she looked equally bad, but was sailing on a pure adrenaline rush. Since Fitch seemed disinclined to any further conversation, she turned her thoughts back to the long talk they'd had as they waited at the motel.

After considerable prodding from her, Fitch had admitted he'd felt all along that something wasn't right about their assignment to Cape Perdido. "And now, with this fire coming on the heels of Eldon's so-called joke about manufacturing dirt on McNear, plus this stuff about investigating Joseph, I'm certain. He wasn't at all interested in the legal issues I discussed with him yesterday afternoon, and he's downright negative about our chances for turning the situation around unless we take drastic — and, to my way of thinking, unethical — measures."

"So why'd he even bother to volunteer our services? Or come out here?"

"I don't know."

"What made you feel there was something funny going on in the first place?"

"Well, for one thing, he could've sent

Abe Reasoner." Fitch named the other water lawyer on ECC's panel of consultants. "Abe is much more experienced than I, and really wanted to come. But instead Eldon picked me. And he didn't want to send you, but had to because everybody else was assigned to long-term projects. He cautioned me against sharing anything more with you than you absolutely needed to know — including his plans to come out here."

So Eldon probably was the one who had removed the memo about his travel plans from her packet. "Did he tell you why he didn't want me?"

Fitch looked uneasy. "More or less."

"He either did, or he didn't."

"All right. He told me that you have a reputation for overzealousness, and he was afraid you'd do something extreme that would discredit the foundation."

"Overzealousness?"

"That's the word he used."

"Did he back this up with any examples?"

"Jess, do we have to go into this now?"

"Yes, we do."

"Okay, if you have to know, Eldon said you'd gotten in trouble while you were with the New York State Department of

Environmental Conservation. Told me you'd gone off on a vendetta against somebody, and the head of your department talked him into hiring you to get you out of their hair."

"That's ridiculous! It wasn't a vendetta."

"What was it?"

"I don't have to explain anything to you."

"Come on, Jess, I'm leveling with you. We've got a bad situation on our hands, and whether you like it or not, we're in it together."

"But it's got nothing to do with . . . All right." She took a deep breath. "What happened in Albany, I was working on wastewater enforcement, and I began to suspect that one of the paint manufacturing firms near Poughkeepsie was illegally disposing of dangerous chemicals. I investigated them very carefully, documented everything, and then I presented my findings to my supervisor. Initially he was excited about going after the firm, but when he brought my report to his boss, he was told not to pursue it. Turned out a state senator's son was an exec with the company and held a large block of stock."

Fitch shrugged. "Doesn't sound like a vendetta to me."

She got up, went over to the balcony door, pulled back the curtain, and peered out at the dark sea. After a moment she said, "There's more."

"Oh?"

"I . . . didn't take their decision very well. So I went to the press. My supervisor found out in time to get the story buried, and that was when I was told to look for another job." As she spoke, she thought of how the notice of the position with ECC had mysteriously appeared in her in-box at work, remembered the ease of her interview with Whitesides, the speed of his offer.

So she hadn't landed the job with ECC on her own; it had been arranged in order to get rid of her. Just as she'd landed the job with the state because of her father's connections, and the job she'd earlier held with a consulting firm in Denver because of a college professor's influence.

Way to go, Jessie. Spend your life riding around on other people's coattails.

But that wasn't a fair assessment. Didn't everybody use connections to get ahead in a world where it was increasingly difficult to make it on your own? Besides, she'd been a hard worker, a conscientious employee —

Another realization struck her, worse

than the first: Whitesides probably intended to keep her on only until he found cause to fire her.

Fitch came up behind her. "You okay?"

She let go of the curtain and turned. "Just kind of blindsided by all this."

"It's a lot to take in, I know."

"Yeah." She crossed to the sofa, sat down heavily. "I don't see any reason why I shouldn't pack up and go home."

"What about Eldon being missing? You can't just —"

"You know what, Fitch? I don't give a shit about Eldon. He can stay missing, for all I care."

"You don't mean that."

"How the hell do you know what I mean?" Her disillusionment boiled over into rage at him. "What do you know about me? You've got it easy, with your law degree and your Benz, and your plans to strike it rich with SoftTech's IPO, and a million friends who seem to want to talk with you on the phone all the time — although God knows why. You have no idea of what it's like to be me!"

Surprisingly, Fitch laughed at her tirade.

"What's so funny?"

"You. Me. Everything." He sank onto the other end of the sofa, shaking his head.

"My law degree is from a second-rate school, and it's only by working my butt off and specializing in an area that's currently in big demand that I've gotten anywhere. If water rights weren't a hot issue these days, I'd probably be sharpening pencils at my uncle's estate-planning firm. The Benz is a twenty-year-old piece of shit that I bought from my older brother, who made it big on Wall Street. I'm probably going to miss the IPO because I won't be able to come up with enough cash. And those friends you heard me talking to? Mainly it was their machines, and you didn't hear them calling back, did you?"

Jessie stared at him.

Fitch smiled crookedly. "Just so long as we're being frank with one another."

"You talk to people's *machines?*"

"Not usually. But when I met you at the airport, I could tell you didn't think much of me, so I tried to impress you. I should've known you weren't the type who cares about those kinds of things."

"You admitting this is pretty impressive."

"Can we start from scratch, then?"

"I'm willing. If we're gonna salvage this situation, we've got to get along."

"Sounds like you've decided to stay."

She weighed her words before she spoke. "We've got the foundation to think of. Whatever Eldon's done — whatever's happened to him — the foundation does good work. Besides, there're a lot of people here who are depending on us."

"Good girl."

"Don't call me a girl, or I'll break your cell phone and you won't be able to reach all those machines that're so eager to hear from you."

Now she waited while the coffee shop waitress filled her cup with more of the vile-tasting brew, then said, "Can I ask you something?"

"Sure. You already know the worst about me."

"Where did you go on the night of the power outage? You said you were meeting with the hydrologist, but when I called him he told me the appointment wasn't till the next morning."

Fitch turned his bleary eyes from the window. "You were checking up on me, huh?"

"Well, you'd already lied about Eldon coming out."

"Okay, the thing was, you were pressuring me, and I had to get away from you. I knew if I went to my room, you'd follow

206

and keep hounding me. So I just drove for a while and then sat at an overlook and watched the waves."

"In the rain?"

"Wasn't so bad."

She studied him, decided he was telling the truth. "So now — what's our best-case scenario about Eldon?"

"We're wrong about him having anything to do with the fire at the mill. He surfaces, and it turns out he was enticed into spending the night with a sexy lady in the next room."

"And worst case?"

"We're right about the fire, and for some reason he's been kidnapped or killed. Or he staged his own disappearance."

"I hadn't thought he might've staged it. But whatever the case is, I don't think we can go this alone."

"Neither do I. But who can we confide in? Who can we trust?"

"I honestly don't know."

Joseph Openshaw

Joseph stepped out of Rose Garza's small prefab home into the foggy morning. Rose, his maternal aunt, followed, shutting the door and hugging her sweater around her stocky body. He had brought the nearly comatose Harold Kosovich to her because she was a retired nurse. By the time he'd tried the emergency services number and, as he'd expected, found it busy, Rose had prepared one of her concoctions, and together they'd managed to save Harold: Rose dosing him with a vile mixture involving charcoal and the native roots whose study she had taken up upon retirement, which caused him to vomit up the liquor and pills; Joseph plying him with gallons of coffee and walking him up and down the hallway of the little house until it was safe to let him sleep. He himself had then slept for a few hours, Rose watching over him as she had countless times when he was a sick child.

Now he was tired and had a headache, and his back hurt from sleeping on the lumpy old sofa. The air, damp and cold, brought with it the faint smell of fire. He tipped his head back and looked up into the misted branches of the nearby redwood grove, trying to free himself of the nightmare aura of his restless dreams, but it clung to him and he shuddered. Rose put a hand on his arm.

"He'll be all right now," she said. "I'll send one of the men up to that shack for his things, and he can stay with me till we arrange for someplace else."

"You know why he was staying there, what happened to his trailer?"

"He sold it, a year or more ago, to a couple who moved up here from Westhaven. Needed the money for his damned liquor, I guess. After that, folks would see him around town, and everybody just assumed he'd gotten a room there. None of us suspected he was living in that shack. If we had, somebody would've done something about it before this."

Joseph nodded. The people on the rez were like that; they didn't have much, but what they did have, they shared.

Rose said, "You okay to drive? You don't look so good."

"I'm okay, just tired."

"You should let me fix you breakfast."

"Couldn't eat. Thanks anyway."

"You don't take care of yourself, living in that goat shed, eating junk food. That what you do in Sacramento?"

"Live in a goat shed, or eat junk food?"

She frowned. "You know what I mean."

"I take care of myself. Don't worry, Rose."

"I worry. Somebody has to, now that your mother's gone to join your father, God forgive him." His mother had died suddenly of a heart attack the previous summer; his father had been killed in a holdup attempt in the county seat, Santa Carla, when Joseph was thirteen.

He didn't respond to the comment. In his opinion, it was not God but Bob Openshaw's dead wife and four widely scattered children from whom his father's soul should beg forgiveness — not that any was likely to be forthcoming. He'd been a drunk, an abuser, and his lifelong laziness and greed had eventually killed him and destroyed his family.

"Joseph?" Rose said. "Don't be a stranger. Come up and let me fix you a meal before you go back to Sacramento. You'll be going back soon, now that this thing with the water bags is over?"

"Over?"

"Well, I just thought . . ." She spread her hands. "Folks around here have made themselves pretty clear, haven't they? It would be foolish for the water board to allow those people to go ahead with their project."

"It's not over, Rose. In fact, I think it's just beginning." Joseph hugged her and loped down the path between her neat borders of pansies before she could ask him what he meant. At the broken pavement he turned right, toward the boarded-up community center, where his van still sat next to Harold's old Buick. He saw no one except a pair of scabrous-looking dogs that lounged on the front stoop of a trailer, tongues lolling. Kosovich's car was unlocked; he opened the passenger door, leaned in, and pocketed the keys that were dangling from the ignition. An odor rose to his nostrils — old upholstery and dampness and something he'd caught a faint trace of at the shack the night before. . . .

Gasoline. And not fumes leaking from the tank.

He leaned in farther, sniffing at the seat. Gas had been spilled there, probably a considerable quantity of it.

You think this could have been arson?

Wouldn't surprise me. The buildings are old

211

and dry. A little accelerant poured in the right places . . .

Joseph looked over the seat back, into the rear. Nothing there except beer cans and an empty whiskey bottle and crumpled food wrappers. He backed out, went around to the trunk, and opened it. Dirty rags, a jack, and four five-gallon gasoline containers. He took each out and shook it.

Empty.

Harold, the arsonist?

Harold?

Steph Pace

Steph looked through the door at the restaurant's dining room, saw that all was under control, then crossed the kitchen and the short hallway to her office, where she sat down at the desk and massaged her temples. The morning had been hellish beyond belief, with customers wanting to talk about nothing but the fire at the mill, and media people, drawn by both the shooting of the water bag and the blaze, only too eager to interview them. Arletta had sermonized all through the lunch prep about it being Timothy McNear's bad karma for his betrayal of the community. The cook, Steph thought, might be a New Age version of her devoutly Catholic mother.

Not that Joella Pace didn't have good cause to wish divine retribution upon McNear. Her best friend, Alice Wells, had had a long-running affair with him and then killed herself when he refused to marry her after his wife's death. Years later, Joella had been vehemently opposed to Steph's going to work as nanny to

213

McNear's grandchildren, but had yielded when her daughter pointed out that the salary was three times what she could have made waitressing and that the schedule would permit her more time to study. And so Steph had gone to live in the big house on the hill and care for Max and Shelby. Max the Meek and Shelby the Sadist, as she'd privately called them. The tragic loss of a mother often brought out different undesirable character traits in siblings.

Should've listened to Mama, she thought now. If only . . .

If only she hadn't gone to work for McNear, if only she hadn't told Joseph and Curtis and Mack what went on in that hilltop house, if only they hadn't been angry and springtime-restless and bored, ready to try anything. Things would be so different now. Mack, with his brother Ike, would be running the ranch in the hills where the Kudge family had grown wine grapes and chestnuts for over a hundred years. Curtis would have established a successful law practice and would also do pro bono work for his people. She and Joseph would have married and moved to one of the far-off cities they'd talked about so often. When they came back to visit Cape Perdido, they would get together with the others and bask happily in the light of their collective accomplishments.

But it hadn't worked out the way they'd planned. In the course of one evening they'd sabotaged their futures. Now Mack was long dead, Curtis trapped in a slipping-down life. And she and Joseph had played out the final act of their love story in a series of confrontations that left both betrayed and forever altered.

I can't see you or touch you without wondering.

Wondering what, Joseph? Are you saying it was my fault?

No, of course not. None of us could've known what would happen.

But that's it, isn't it? None of us really knows what did *happen. Except Mack, and he can't tell.*

I believe you when you say —

Do you? Because I'm not sure I believe you.

Secrets. Half-truths. Outright lies. They lived inside her like a virus, normally under control, but subject to violent flare-ups. The prospect of those flare-ups had ruled her life, dictated her every action and reaction. Now, no matter what the risk, it was time for a cure.

Steph picked up the phone receiver and dialed McNear's well-remembered number.

Timothy McNear

Timothy was anxious and depressed when he returned home after his meeting with the fire marshal and the sheriff's department and the insurance investigators at the mill. The fire's origin had already been determined to be arson, and although they had been polite and respectful toward him, he knew he was their prime suspect. The light on his answering machine was flashing, and his spirits improved somewhat when he played Stephanie Pace's message.

She had agreed to meet with him at four that afternoon, and her choice of a meeting place was a good one: the rhododendron preserve south of Signal Port. A busy tourist attraction during the spring blooming season, but relatively deserted this time of year — staffed by a caretaker, however, who collected a nominal fee when he opened the gate to visitors. To him, Timothy and Stephanie would merely be acquaintances who had arrived separately and met on the path, but his presence would reassure her as to her safety.

Clever girl, but she doesn't know that I could never harm her. And maybe that's all to the good.

Of course, he never *would* harm her. Not again, not intentionally.

Briefly he pictured her as a child: the smiley, curly-haired little girl riding around on her father's shoulders at the mill's annual picnic. As a teenager: awkward, leggy, nervously balancing plates at her first summer job down at Tai Haruru. As a young adult: an almond-eyed beauty, nodding shyly at him when he entered the kitchen, where she was trying to coax his grandsons into eating their Wheaties.

Ah, Jesus!

His decision to provide a nanny for the boys wasn't an entirely selfish one: Stephanie's father had died when his pickup skidded on the rain-slick pavement of the coast highway and went over the cliffs down at Deer Harbor; his life insurance was barely enough to pay off the mortgage on the family home, and Timothy had heard that Stephanie was working two waitressing jobs to help her mother make ends meet. So he'd offered her more than the going rate for child-care workers, to live in his servants' quarters and care for the boys. She'd been good with them.

Throughout the hot summer and autumn, the wretched rainy winter, and part of the lovely spring, Stephanie had kept nine-year-old Max and twelve-year-old Shelby amused, distracting them from their grief over their mother. She'd concocted games for them, asked Timothy to let them use the potting shed in the garden for a playhouse. The boys had minded her, respectfully calling her Miss Stephanie, but they'd also regarded her as a friend.

Should have had children of her own. That would have been the normal course of events. But after the night of June 30, 1984, nothing was normal for any of us again.

And nothing will be normal again after this afternoon.

Timothy forced his mind away from the past and future. No more woolgathering. He had an essential stop to make before he began the drive south.

Jessie Domingo

Jessie returned to the Shorebird alone at a little after noon, Fitch having volunteered to remain at the Tides Inn in case Eldon surfaced. She sensed that he didn't really believe that was likely but wanted to be alone for a time while he struggled to come to terms with the day's discoveries. She certainly couldn't fault him for that; her own mind and body were on overload, and she needed to rest before she considered what to do next.

Phone messages had been slipped under her door: from Bernina, wanting to meet for lunch; from two of the Friends, saying they had questions for her; from reporters for the county TV station and the Santa Carla paper wanting to interview her; from Joseph, asking that she call him. She reserved the messages from the Friends and the media for later, discarded the slip with Bernina's number on it. At the meeting with Whitesides yesterday afternoon, she'd been disturbed by Bernina's acceptance of his underhanded tactics, and she didn't want to see the woman until she'd had time to process her reaction. The message from Joseph she fingered nervously. She and Fitch still had not decided whom they could trust with the news of Eldon's disappearance, but given the detective's report on Joseph that they'd found saved on Eldon's computer, he was far down on their list.

The report had detailed Joseph's career as an environmentalist and activist since his student days at Berkeley: Phi Beta Kappa graduate with a tendency to get in trouble with the law at protests; internship with the state environmental protection agency; paid positions with various pro-environment organizations, most recently as director of the California Coalition for Environmental Preservation, a powerful group that encompassed a wide spectrum of organizations working to preserve the state's natural resources. Joseph's two books were used as supplemental texts at universities across the country and he had received numerous awards and citations.

No stain had touched Joseph's reputation until the previous spring, when $150,000 went missing from the Coalition's general fund. Although there was no evidence he had committed the crime, and few details had appeared in the press, the Coalition's board of directors called into question his ability to lead effectively, and in May he had quietly resigned. Yet Eldon must have sensed something more, or else why had he told the investigator to continue?

Damn, this wasn't right! Jessie had known Joseph by reputation since college, had read both his books. Neither the man behind those words nor the individual she'd come to know personally struck her as a thief, or even as an inept manager. Why not give him the chance to defend himself?

His message, left a little over an hour ago, asked her to call him at home. At the Friends' meeting on the night Jessie arrived in Cape Perdido, Bernina had pointed out the former animal shed in her backyard that had been converted to a studio apartment, said that Joseph was living there. Jessie decided to take a brief nap, then pay him a visit.

The tiny structure where Joseph lived looked as if it had been built from scrap lumber; its roof was tar paper, its windows encased in cheap aluminum frames. Someone — probably Bernina — had attempted to beautify it by planting shrubs with bright red berries on either side of the door, but they failed to detract from the uneven joints and mismatched boards.

When Joseph answered her knock, Jessie was shocked at how bad he looked; overnight he seemed to have aged ten years. As he motioned her inside, he clawed at his silver-gray curls, ran a hand over the stubble on his chin. Then he looked around and began straightening the comforter on the single bed.

"I don't usually have visitors here," he said. "I'm not really set up for them."

An understatement. Besides the bed, there was a bookcase, a table set up as an office, and a single typist's chair. The room felt claustrophobic in the extreme.

Jessie said, "We could go get a cup of coffee or a drink."

"If you don't mind staying here, it would be better. We need to talk privately."

"Fine with me." She swiveled the chair away from the computer and sat, while he took a place on the edge of the bed.

"Eldon —" she began.

"The fire —" he said at the same time.

"Go ahead."

"No, you first, please."

She started over. "Eldon's had an investigator gathering background on you. He knows about the embezzlement at the

California Coalition." When he didn't immediately react, she added, "You don't seem surprised."

"I know someone's been making inquiries."

"The investigator's report seems pretty straightforward, but Eldon asked him to keep digging. Why, d'you suppose?"

Joseph shrugged. "He's just being Eldon."

"Meaning?"

"How do I put this? Eldon likes to be in control, and he doesn't share the spotlight with anyone. I think he came out here with the idea of coercing Timothy McNear into going back on his agreement with Aqueduct, then taking credit for engineering a settlement. Diplomacy always makes one look good with corporate backers like his."

"But why does he want to get something on *you?*"

"Because I'm the loose cannon in his plans. He's counting on the Friends, and in particular Bernina — who, as you must have noticed, is completely won over — to go along with whatever he wants to do. He's got Fitch jumping at his every request. You, he's not so sure of, but he figures he can handle you somehow. But me — he knows he can't control me. We have a long history of conflict. So he's trying to dig up some dirt that'll give him leverage, just as he hopes to with Timothy McNear."

"*Is* there any dirt?"

He smiled faintly. "My, you're direct. No, there isn't. The money disappeared. No one's been able to figure out what happened. I didn't take it, and I don't know who did."

"But you resigned."

"Because I couldn't do a good job under a cloud of suspicion, and I cared enough about the organization to put it in the hands of someone who would be effective."

Jessie nodded. She'd always been able to recognize a truth-teller, and Joseph was one. He was also the person she could confide in. "Okay, there's something more I have to tell you: Eldon's disappeared." She recounted what she and Fitch had found at the Tides Inn. "Neither of us knows what to do," she finished, "especially since we think he had some connection with the fire at the mill."

Joseph frowned. "Why?"

"His entire approach to the situation. Talking about getting dirt on McNear, his disinterest in going through legal channels. I gather he's used such tactics before."

"Well, yes, but I doubt even Eldon

would resort to arson. Besides . . ." He hesitated.

"Besides?"

"This is to go no farther than this room, d'you understand?"

"Yes."

"I know who set the fire. You remember Harold Kosovich?"

"The little man who used to work at the mill."

"Right. I saw him at the fire and followed him to a shack on the rez, where he's been living. Found him overdosing on booze and pills. He's okay now, but there were empty gas containers in the trunk of his car."

"But why would *he* set the fire?"

"There's a lot of . . . stuff twisted up in Harold's mind, I think. His auto accident, being shunted off into administration, losing his job, and more recently, losing his trailer. He's been fixated on the mill since it closed. This water-bag thing probably pushed him over the edge."

"But setting that fire wasn't a sudden impulse. He would've had to buy the gasoline, plan for a time when there was nobody around. Plan how to set it so he wouldn't be trapped and killed."

"Well, Harold knows the mill. I suspect

he's been slipping in and out of there for a long time — not doing any harm, just mourning the past."

With some relief, Jessie let go of the notion that Eldon had hired an arsonist. "So are you going to the sheriff with this?"

"Not till I can talk with Harold and confirm my suspicions. And even then I don't know what I'll do. He's disturbed, that's for sure, but what's the good in having him arrested and put away? He's with my aunt on the rez, and she'll look out for him; other folks will as well. I'm tempted to let things lie."

"Well, it's your call. Now, what do you think we should do about Eldon?"

"First you should alert the sheriff's department. Because he's a stranger to the area and the circumstances are suspicious, they'll put out a be-on-the-lookout order right away. In the meantime, I'll ask around. I've got some contacts who might be able to shed some light on this."

Jessie nodded, glad to have placed the matter in Joseph's capable hands.

Joseph Openshaw

The Kudge ranch spread over 260 acres on the ridge above Calvert's Landing. Joseph hadn't visited it in over twenty years, and as he drove in through the wooden gate, he saw that the vineyards lining the drive were poorly tended; a quarter mile later the big frame house came into view, its white paint faded and blistering, front porch sagging. The rosebushes that Doris Kudge, Mack and Ike's mother, had carefully nurtured were woody and choked with weeds. Probably the chestnut trees in the orchards that stretched beyond the house were in a similar state of neglect.

Well, that was no surprise. Joseph had heard that Ike had let the place go since his parents died. Heard also that he'd turned his hand to cooking meth and had taken up with a rough crowd.

He got out of his van and went up on the house's sagging front porch. The afternoon was warm here on the ridge, and the door was open behind the screen; he knocked, then called out. After a moment Ike appeared at the end of the long hall, wearing cutoff jeans and a stained T-shirt that strained at his gut, and carrying a can of Bud.

"Joseph?" he said. "What the hell're you doing here?"

Ike's tone wasn't unfriendly, so Joseph opened the screen door and stepped inside. An odor assailed him: not meth — the factory would be far from the house — but a mixture of mildew, wet dog, grease, and cat piss. When Joseph had visited his friend Mack here, the house had always smelled of lemon polish and baking.

"Hey," Ike added, "you want a beer?"

"Sure." Joseph followed him down the hallway to the kitchen at the rear. The greasy odor was more pronounced there, and the countertops were covered with dirty dishes, beer cans, and take-out cartons. Ike got another Bud from the fridge and tossed it to Joseph, cleared a stack of newspapers from a chair at the round table, and motioned for him to sit.

"Been a while," he said. "I seen you up on the platform at the mill the other day. Guess you heard me pretty good."

"Yeah. You sure were giving those waterbaggers hell."

"You bet. They piss me off so damn

much. They goin' away now that the mill's burned down?"

"Doubt it."

"Shit, after that fire, you'd think they'd get the message."

"You think the fire was meant as a message?"

"Had to be. The timing, you know."

"Well, I doubt the message got across. They want what they want, and they're probably going to pursue the project."

"Fuckin' outsiders! What right — ah, hell, don't get me started. So why'd you come up here, anyway? It ain't like we're buddies, never was."

"I've got a problem, and I think you can help me. A man who's on our side of this water grab issue has gone missing. Name's Eldon Whitesides, from New York City, and he disappeared from the Tides Inn sometime between nine last night and three this morning."

"Why you think I can help you?"

"I hear you've got connections."

"With people who can make somebody disappear?" Ike crumpled his beer can and went to get another. "You been listening to too many rumors, Joseph."

"Rumors nearly always have some basis in fact."

"Maybe so." Ike sat down heavily. "You know, when you were hanging with Mack, I never liked you. You always had this way of acting better than the rest of us. I don't much like you now, but I like what you're trying to do for the river. So I'll ask around, okay?"

"Thanks, Ike."

"Don't thank me yet. I ain't guaranteeing nothing."

"I know that. And thanks for the beer." Joseph stood.

Ike watched him, eyes narrowed. "Guess you're surprised to see what shape the place is in."

"Yeah, I am."

"I just couldn't cut it after Ma and Pa died. I'm not much of a rancher, I guess. Maybe if Mack was alive, we could've kept things going, but then if he hadn't died, Ma and Pa would probably still be here."

Something cold moved inside Joseph. "How d'you figure that?"

"Because Mack was their favorite, and they never got over him dying. Pa had a bad heart, but not that bad. After Mack, he just gave up on living. And Ma, she killed herself. Pills."

"I didn't know that."

"Nobody knew. The doc put it down as an accidental overdose, so she could be buried in the Catholic cemetery, but I knew different. She just didn't want to go on without the two of them."

One more burden to bear. Would it never end?

Steph Pace

Steph was inventorying liquor behind the bar and brooding about her four o'clock appointment with Timothy McNear when the door opened and Neil Woodsman came in. "We're not open till five," she called out, but the man crossed toward her and sat down on a stool.

"I know," he said, "but I was hoping you'd bend the rules, join me in a drink."

As a businesswoman, she felt she should be polite to him. As a native of the Cape, she'd like to smack that look of smug self-confidence off his bearded face.

"I'm sorry —"

"Please, just one round."

Then again, maybe she could find out what the waterbaggers' plans were. Joseph would thank her for doing a bit of detective work. "All right, one," she said, and poured from the bottle he indicated, then took down a wineglass for herself. Medicinal, she thought.

"Where's Mr. Erickson?" she asked.

"Gregory's down at the mill, talking with the waste management people about the best way to dispose of the waterbag."

"You people planning on pursuing your project?"

"Why not?"

"Well, if I were you, I'd be afraid of more violent incidents. The community's made it pretty clear they don't want you here."

"Once the project's off the ground, they'll forget they ever opposed it."

"I don't think so. And the state water board may take our wishes into consideration. Or feel the situation here is too volatile to grant your application."

He shrugged. "I guess we'll just have to wait and see."

"Doesn't it concern you that down the line people might sabotage your pipelines or continue to shoot up the bags?"

"Not particularly. Like I said, the opposition will go away in time."

"And the mill burning down — that doesn't alter anything?"

"I very much doubt the fire had anything to do with our project. But now Timothy McNear will have to clear the site, and that'll make it easier for us to go in there to trench and lay pipe."

"You can't believe it was coincidence that the mill burned a day after the bag was shot?"

Again he shrugged.

She said, "Well, I don't think it's coincidence, and neither do any of the people I've heard talking about it. How much did you pay McNear to allow you a right-of-way across the land?"

Woodsman's eyes glittered. Something disconcerting and oddly familiar there. She'd seen a look like that before. He rolled his glass between his fingers for a moment, then sipped. "Enough."

"And why'd you target the Perdido? Why not the Mad River, up in Humboldt County, or the Albion or Gualala, down in Mendocino?"

"Another firm is interested in those. Besides, the geographical situation here is perfect for our purposes — the river, the point with a natural harbor. And, of course, there's McNear." His lip curled when he said the name.

"You targeted him because you knew he'd shut down the mill and probably needed the money."

Woodsman nodded.

Steph's fingers tensed on her glass, the urge to smack him coming on even stronger.

He grinned widely, taking pleasure in her poorly concealed anger. "It's just business, Miss Stephanie," he said. "Just good business."

Timothy McNear

Timothy sat in his car in the parking lot of the small electronics shop in Calvert's Landing, examining the tiny voice-activated tape recorder that he'd just bought. How long since he'd used such a device? Five years, anyway, before he'd closed the mill. Weren't these things supposed to get simpler as the technology improved? It was no larger than a cigarette pack, but the instructions booklet was a quarter inch thick, with text that he was sure was equally incomprehensible in English, Spanish, and French.

It took a few moments to figure out the basic operation, and then he discovered that the batteries were not included. Back into the store for those. Then he had to test the recording volume, adjust and readjust, and next there was the question of where on his person to conceal it. Would it be too obvious in the breast pocket of his flannel shirt? No. Well, then, he was ready for his meeting.

Timothy was no stranger to clandestine recordings. Once he'd conceded that the business world, not academia, was to be his lifetime habitat, he was consumed with a desire to succeed. Even in those days of clumsy reel-to-reel technology, he had secretly taped meetings and negotiations, later playing and replaying them, looking for ways he might refine his technique. Not that it had needed much improvement — the man who had thought of himself as bookish and introverted found he was articulate and diplomatic, as well as a tough adversary when necessary. His quick mind could expose the fallacies behind what appeared to be logical arguments, and his sharp tongue could wither the most experienced union negotiators with a few well-chosen words.

Extracting the information he wanted from Stephanie Pace would pose no problem for a man like him. And he'd have his tape as evidence in case she later refused to cooperate in his plan.

Jessie Domingo

Jessie watched as the sheriff's department detective who had introduced herself as Rhoda Swift examined Eldon Whitesides's wallet. Swift was fine-featured and dark-haired, dressed in tan slacks and a brown sweater rather than a uniform; her handshake indicated strength that Jessie didn't usually associate with a woman of her small stature.

Swift stared meditatively at Eldon's driver's license, counted the bills stored in the compartment behind it. "You were right to call us," she said. "There're bloodstains on the corner of that coffee table. I'm going to declare this room a crime scene and get my technicians out here."

Fitch, who was seated on the sofa, gave a faint sigh.

"I'll need to take formal statements from both of you," Swift added, "but that can wait till tomorrow morning. Right now I want to secure the scene and call in my people."

Jessie glanced at Eldon's laptop, where it still rested on the table. "His computer —" she began.

"Is part of the scene." Swift opened the door and motioned them out. "The substation is on Center Street," she said. "Drop in any time tomorrow morning and we'll get those statements."

Jessie followed Fitch down the stairs and across the parking area. When they reached the car, she said in a low voice, "The stuff about Joseph on the computer —"

"Let them read it and question him."

"But I told you what he said."

"That's *his* story."

"What, you think he lied to me?"

"Maybe he told the truth, maybe not. But you strike me as altogether too willing to believe him."

"You mean I strike you as naive."

"I didn't say that."

"You didn't have to."

Fitch held out his hand. "Give me the car keys."

"Why?"

"Because, as usual, you're getting overwrought. We'll be safer if I'm the one behind the wheel."

So much for detente with Fitch. She slapped the keys into his hand and climbed in on the passenger side.

As Fitch drove slowly through Calvert's Landing, then picked up speed on the highway, Jessie fumed inwardly. But as the miles slipped by, her self-awareness asserted itself, and she began to consider what he had said. *Was* she too trusting, merely because Joseph had long been one of her icons? Was she indeed naive?

In Boulder she'd developed a crush on her geology professor and had an affair with him, mistaking his being flattered by a young woman's attention for real feeling. But at graduation time he'd eased her out of his life by recommending her for a job in Denver. It had taken a year to get over the pain of that rejection, and her job had been eliminated within eighteen months. Then, in Albany, her idealistic and impetuous actions had almost destroyed her career. Later, she'd believed that Eldon Whitesides had hired her on her own merits. Well, look at the truth of that situation.

When're you going to grow up, Jessie?
Maybe now's the time.

She glanced at Fitch. He was driving with both hands clamped on the wheel, his jaw bulging as if he was grinding his teeth.

"Hey," she said, "you could be right. Maybe I am cutting Joseph too much slack."

He relaxed some. "And maybe you have better people instincts than I. I'm a skeptic by nature."

"So what should we do next?"

"It's too late now, but tomorrow one of us should call the people on the foundation's board, alert them to what's happened. And we'll call a meeting of the Friends' board, fill them in, try to reassure them."

"What about Eldon?"

"It's in the hands of the sheriff's department. Leave it there."

When Jessie was silent, he added, "I mean it, Jess. Back off and let them do their job."

"Okay," she said. But then, in a gesture she hadn't used since childhood, she crossed her fingers against the lie.

Joseph Openshaw

Rose Garza's face was strained as she admitted Joseph to her small house. She must be exhausted from taking care of Harold Kosovich all night, he thought. Rose had spent her life tending to others and shouldn't have to be so burdened in her retirement. But then, she wouldn't be content if she wasn't helping someone in need.

"How's Harold?" he asked.

"He's gone."

"Gone where? Back to that shack? His car's still parked at the community center."

Rose took his hand, went to the sofa, and pulled him down beside her. "Not that kind of gone. He died a few hours ago. His heart just gave out."

At first Joseph couldn't take it in. The little man had been resting comfortably when he'd left that morning. Now he'd never know for sure if Harold had set the fire.

Rose added, "All those years of heavy drinking, using whatever prescription drugs he could get his hands on, he didn't have the strength to survive this last episode. Maybe he's better off."

"Nobody's better off dead." But as he spoke, he knew the words were untrue. Harold was a tortured man and tired of living; such a man would always find a way out, and it was an unkindness to hinder his departure.

Rose didn't respond to his statement. "The people here on the rez will take care of his burial," she said. "Tom and Gina Mallon have donated a space in their plot in the graveyard."

Joseph pictured the cemetery in the redwood grove beyond the community center: small, with well-tended graves topped by modest markers. There were worse places to spend eternity.

"Joey?" Rose said, using the diminutive no one had called him by since childhood. "D'you suppose it was losing his trailer made him do it?"

Right then and there he knew he'd never share his suspicions about Harold's starting the fire.

"I saw him at the mill last night, watching it burn. That place was his last connection to the days when he was reasonably happy; its loss must've been too much for him."

Rose nodded, accepting the explanation without question, then sighed deeply, pressing his hand.

They'll remember you as a sad, broken man, Harold. But I'm damned if I'll let them remember you as an arsonist.

Steph Pace

Steph started along the path through the rhododendron grove. It wound uphill in a series of gentle rises interspersed with steeper flights of stone steps and would, she knew, eventually loop back to the parking lot below. The rhodos, many more than twelve feet tall, grew to either side, their branches tipped with new growth. In another month or so the buds would form, and by May the brilliant flowers — deep purple, lavender-blue, red, pink, and white — would lure scores of visitors. But now the preserve was drab and deserted.

Midway up, the path crossed a hump-backed bridge over a stream that ran fast and clear, surging around the rocks in its bed. Steph stopped, leaned over the side, and watched the water. It was cold here in the grove, and mist draped the rhodos' topmost branches. Cold inside her, too.

She was afraid, even though she'd made it a point to speak with the caretaker, told him she would be back near closing time, and knew he would come looking for her if she didn't appear. Somewhere up ahead Timothy McNear waited; she had seen his Lincoln, the only other car in the parking area. She'd feared him since she was a teenager, and she was probably a fool to have obeyed his summons.

Too late now. After a moment she gathered her courage, squared her shoulders, and continued up the path.

At its top, just before it looped back downhill, she spotted McNear hunched on a stone bench, wearing a tan wool shirt and cords. He leaned forward, elbows on his knees, hands dangling between them. Her fear didn't exactly leave her, but it eased some, and she thought, My God, he's such a sad-looking old man!

McNear heard her approach and stood. "Miss Stephanie," he said, "I was afraid you'd changed your mind about meeting me."

"No," she said, "I was delayed at the restaurant."

McNear indicated that she should sit and resumed his place. He was too close, and she could feel his body heat. Quickly she shifted away, but the bench was small and she couldn't put enough space between them. He seemed oblivious to her discomfort.

He said, "You know why I wanted to meet with you."

"I assume to talk about . . . that night."

"June thirtieth, nineteen-eighty-four."

"Why, after all this time?"

"Because the past has an unfortunate habit of resurrecting itself and disrupting the present. The waterbaggers are holding the events of that night over my head. That's why I gave them the right-of-way across my land."

A chill descended on Steph's shoulders. "But how can they possibly know anything?"

"They claim they have an eyewitness to me moving Mack Kudge's body from my garden to the pier at the mill. Someone who told them about it in detail. It could only be one of three people: you, Joseph Openshaw, or Curtis Hope. If I can identify the person and persuade him to recant his story, the waterbaggers can be stopped, and our river and community saved."

Me, Joseph, or Curtis. The other night when Joseph came to the house, he said he thought Curt was out of control, but I can't imagine him going so far as to help the waterbaggers.

She asked, "Why the change of heart at this point?"

McNear's gaze grew remote. "It's something I can't explain to someone as young as you."

"Young? I haven't felt young in twenty years. Try me."

"Suffice it to say that I don't want to be remembered as the man who ruined Cape Perdido — twice. So, Miss Stephanie, are you the one who betrayed me?"

"I barely know Woodsman or Erickson. Besides, I don't really know what you did that night. I'm sure Joseph doesn't, either. Curtis . . . I couldn't say."

McNear frowned. "Surely you've discussed it with them."

"Joseph and I didn't say a word about it from shortly after it happened until a couple of days ago. And Curtis has never discussed it."

"I find that hard to believe."

"Do you, Mr. McNear? Think about it. When was the last time *you* discussed it with anybody?"

Timothy McNear

Timothy stared at Stephanie Pace, trying to adjust the concept he'd held in his mind all these years to the one she'd just presented. After a moment he said, "Perhaps you should tell me what you remember."

A look akin to panic passed over her face. "Is this really necessary?"

"Yes, it is."

"Okay." A deep, nervous breath. "When I was working for you, I mentioned to Joseph and Curtis and Mack about all the expensive things you had, and the cash you kept in the study. And after you . . . after I quit and told them the reason why, they were angry and wanted to get back at you. So we decided to burglarize your house. It was a stupid thing to do, but we were young and impetuous . . . and, oh God, I wish none of it had ever happened!"

The reason why. A harmless pass at a beautiful young woman. Well, harmless to a middle-aged reprobate like me; attempted rape to her.

"Miss Stephanie, if I could go back in time —"

"Doesn't matter now." She slashed her hand through the air, a swift, negating gesture.

She doesn't want my apology; just wants to get this over with. Well, no more than I.

"Go on with your story," he said.

"We'd heard Robert was taking the boys to San Francisco to catch their ship for Australia, and we'd seen in the paper that you were addressing a lumber industry trade association in Sacramento that same night. The house would be empty. I still had my key, so we didn't really have to break in."

"Weren't you afraid you'd be the obvious suspect in a burglary?"

"I knew you'd suspect me, but I didn't think you'd tell the sheriff. You wouldn't want anyone to find out what you'd tried to do to me." She smiled painfully. "And I was right, wasn't I? You never reported the theft, and Mack's body turned up on the pier at your lumberyard, rather than in your garden."

He pictured himself going to the potting shed in the far reaches of the garden for a wheelbarrow and tarp. Trundling the body to the garage, loading it into his car. The nightmarish drive through the thick fog. Circumventing his own security force. The awkwardness of Mack Kudge's dead weight as he carried him along the pier . . .

"Go on."

"As soon as we were inside the house, we got spooked, realized that we were in over our heads, but none of us dared back down and lose face. Mack and I were in the study when I thought I heard someone upstairs. We'd decided that if anything went wrong, we'd split up and meet later at the beach at Cauldron Creek, so he and I stuffed the money into my tote bag and left by the door to the garden. I had the bag, was well ahead of him, was halfway to the rear wall when I realized he wasn't behind me anymore. Then, when I got to the wall, I heard a shot. I ran, caught a ride on the highway with a passing tourist, went to the beach, and waited. A little while later, Curt and Joseph showed up. They'd been in separate parts of the house when they heard the shot, ran into the garden, and found Mack's body. So they left everything and took off."

Stephanie's voice had gone shrill while reliving the night. To calm her, Timothy put a hand on her arm, but she pulled away as if it were red-hot.

"Were any of you armed?" he asked.

"I didn't think so at the time. All of us

owned guns: the guys were hunters; I had inherited my father's old twenty-two and was a good shot. But we made a pact before we went up there: no weapons."

"But now you suspect someone didn't honor it?"

She looked away from him.

"Well?"

". . . I suspected someone had brought a gun almost from the first. And later Joseph let slip that he thought I might have panicked and shot Mack by accident. Curtis wouldn't talk about it — ever. That's what drove the three of us apart. Suspicion."

"And from the vantage of the present, what do you think happened?"

She closed her eyes, put her fingers to her lips.

Timothy waited.

"Joseph came to see me the other night. Since he's been back, he's insisted we not talk about what happened, but he finally admitted he's constantly thinking about it. And he's worried about Curtis. He made me go over what I remember in detail; then he did the same."

"And?"

"He remembered that he and Curtis didn't come upon Mack's body at the same time. Curtis was in the garden standing over it when Joseph came out of the house."

A very different scenario than I imagined.

To make the seed of suspicion Joseph had already planted in her mind grow, Timothy said, "So you think Curtis may have been the one who accidentally shot Mack. And he may be trying to put his crime on me by claiming to be an eyewitness."

"Why would he do that, after all these years?"

Timothy shrugged. "Why does anyone do anything?"

And there it is: a way out. Give them Curtis Hope. Admit to concealing a burglary and moving a dead body. Admit to being a fool for a young woman. Admit to trying to save your reputation.

Admit most, but not all, of the truth.

Jessie Domingo

As soon as the door to Fitch's room closed and she heard him on the phone — presumably talking to one of those many machines — Jessie slipped back outside and headed for the far wing of the motel, where the waterbaggers were staying. A maid's cart was parked in front of one of their rooms, and the woman who on the night of the power outage had introduced herself as Nita Bynum was stripping the queen-size bed.

Jessie stepped inside and asked, "Is this Mr. Erickson's room?"

"It was. He's checked out."

"Oh? The others, too?"

"Two of them. Mr. Woodsman's still here."

"Which is his room?"

"Next door." Nita gestured to the left. "But he's not in. I ran into him when he was leaving."

"He say where he was going?"

"Asked if there was anyplace to eat around here besides the Blue Moon. Said he was sick of the same old menu. I told him to try the Oceansong. They do a pretty good burger."

"That's the place on the bluff, up by the volunteer fire department?"

"Right. You're looking for Mr. Woodsman, you'll probably find him there."

The Oceansong was aimed at the tourist: a pit fireplace with a gas jet and fake logs opposite an expanse of windows overlooking a deck and the sea. Long bar and little tables, a chalkboard scrawled with offerings such as popcorn shrimp, nachos, and chicken strips. The deck was closed, its umbrellas battened against the wind; fog was rolling in, a thick bank of it, bringing the night on early. Jessie scanned the room, spotted Woodsman at the bar, just saying good-bye to one of the TV people she'd seen around town. She went over and slipped onto the stool next to him.

He glanced at her, then raised his eyebrows. "Ms. Domingo. We haven't met, but I know you by sight."

"And I know you, too, Mr. Woodsman."

"Neil."

"Jessie."

"May I buy you a drink? I don't suppose

there's anything that says we can't associate with the opposition."

"None at all. I'll take an IPA, if they
have one."

"I'm sure they do." He motioned at a
sign on the backbar: "Largest Selection of
Premium Beers on the North Coast."

After the bartender had taken her order,
Woodsman asked, "So what brings you
here on a foggy evening?"

"I'm tired of eating at the Blue Moon.
Someone told me this place does a good
burger."

"You must've been talking with Nita
Bynum. She steered me here, too. The
Blue Moon's okay, but it's a limited menu,
and I've about worked my way through it."

"I understand the others in your party
have left."

"Only temporarily. There's some
problem with the documents we filed with
the state water board, and they've gone to
Sacramento to address it. I remained behind to deal with the water bag removal
and the media. Can't get away from the reporters. That one" — he motioned to the
man he'd been talking with, who was now
seated near the windows — "followed me
here."

"When's the bag being removed?"

"Tomorrow or the next day. The waste management company is going to tow it to sea and scuttle it."

As the bartender arranged a napkin and glass in front of Jessie, she studied Neil Woodsman. He was probably in his early thirties, good-looking in a rough, outdoorsman's way. His accent was British but somewhat twangy and nasal. Cockney, perhaps?

"Thanks, mate," he said to the bartender, and toasted her.

"So, Neil," she said, "where do you live in North Carolina?"

"Raleigh, but I've lived all over the world, most recently the UK."

"And you've worked for Aqueduct Systems how long?"

"A year."

"Is your educational background in resources management?"

Woodsman smiled. "Are you interrogating me?"

"Just interested."

"I feel as if I were in the witness box."

Slow down, Jessie. Go easy on the personal stuff.

"Sorry. The reason I asked is that most of the people on the staff of my foundation have that background, in some cases coupled with law or business. Take Eldon Whitesides, for example — do you know of him?"

"I don't think so."

"He's our director, flew out yesterday. I thought he might have contacted you people."

"Why would he do that?"

"Eldon's very direct. When he wants to know what the opposition's up to, he's likely to just ask them."

"Well, maybe he contacted Gregory, but if he did, I haven't heard of it."

Jessie sipped beer, tried another tack. "So tell me, what do you think of Cape Perdido?"

"A boring place to visit, and I wouldn't want to live here."

"The people —"

"Are typical of people in small towns. Narrow-minded, provincial, suspicious of outsiders, resistant to progress. I've always hated places like this."

The vehemence behind his words startled Jessie. "Did you live in small towns while you were growing up?"

"I've seen my share."

"They must've been pretty bad."

"Why do you say that?"

"Well, your condemnation of a town and

257

people you've known less than a week has got to be coming from somewhere."

Woodsman looked at his watch and downed the rest of his drink. "It's been nice talking with you," he said, "but I have some calls to make."

"I thought you wanted to get something to eat."

"I'll buy a sandwich at the deli." He dropped some bills on the bar, then crossed the room and pushed out the door.

Jessie watched it swing shut with narrowed eyes. Something had pushed his buttons. She stood, and by the time she got outside, Woodsman's figure was a distant shadow on the road's shoulder, heading toward the motel. She got into her car, waited for a logging truck to pass before she pulled out of the lot; soon its high beams showed Woodsman cutting across the ice plants in front of the motel.

Jessie drove onto the shoulder and idled there, watching Woodsman enter his motel room. She waited a minute or two, deliberating what to do next, and was about to pull back onto the road when he came out again. He went to a white compact that was parked near his unit, slid inside, started it up, and turned north on the highway. Jessie ducked down as he passed her.

Calls to make, my ass!

As she followed, Woodsman kept the car at a steady fifty-five, following the highway toward Oilville and the airport. After a mile or so he turned right into the hills on a poorly paved secondary road. She had to hold back so her headlights wouldn't alert Woodsman that she was behind him, and after a few miles she realized she'd lost him. He could have turned into any one of the lanes that led off into pastureland to distant houses.

She slowed, looking for a place to turn around, swung off the broken pavement into a packed-gravel semicircle, then back onto the road.

Headlight beams came around the curve on the uphill side, and a light-colored vehicle rushed toward her, going much too fast.

Joseph Openshaw

Joseph slammed on his brakes and skidded onto the shoulder when he spotted the car nose-down in the ditch, its headlights shining onto reeds and dead blackberry vines. He pulled on the emergency brake, got out and trotted over, scrambled down the slope to peer through the driver's-side door.

Jessie Domingo sat grasping the wheel of the stalled car, her head bent forward.

"My God!" he exclaimed, and pulled the door open. "Jessie, are you all right?"

"Joseph?" Her voice was thin, shaky.

"Yeah, it's me. What the hell happened?"

"I was trying to turn around." She let go of the wheel, looked up at him. No blood, no visible injuries. "Somebody came around the curve too fast, and I panicked. Hit the accelerator and . . . here I am."

He reached inside and helped her unfasten her seat belt, guided her from the car, and got her leaning up against it. "You hurt?"

"Banged my forehead, but I'll be okay. The car —"

"We'll have to get a tow truck to pull it out of the ditch. My van doesn't have enough power."

"Oh, God, Fitch is gonna kill me! He hates the way I drive."

"Well, you shouldn't've turned across the road on a blind curve."

She pressed her hand to her forehead. "I didn't even *see* the curve. And please don't you start on me. I feel bad enough, and I'm gonna get an earful from Fitch later on."

He turned off her car's lights, took the keys from its ignition, slammed the door, and helped her up to the road. She leaned heavily on him, and he feared that she might be more badly injured than she claimed. As he buckled her into the passenger side of his van, he said, "What were you doing up here, anyway?"

She closed her eyes. "Give me a few minutes, okay?"

"You should see a doctor —"

"No doctor. I'm fine."

"Okay, whatever you say." Briefly he considered taking her to Rose to be checked over. He'd just come from there after having dinner and then helping his aunt complete the arrangements for Harold Kosovich's burial. No, he decided, he'd brought enough trouble to her doorstep in the past twenty-four hours. Instead he drove downhill and then south on the highway, heading for the Blue Moon and Steph.

Steph wasn't at the restaurant, however, and even though business was light, Arletta, Tony, and the Puska twins were frantic. While Joseph got Jessie settled in the bar area with a glass of water and a towel full of ice to apply to her head, Kat Puska kept up a steady complaint about her employer's absence.

"Until Sunday, the woman practically lived here twenty-four seven, and then that morning she takes off to go to the Friends' meeting in the middle of the breakfast service. That night she's gone for dinner, and today she took off at three, told Arletta she'd try to get back by six. Acted damn secretive, too. Six-thirty now, and she's a no-show. Not at home, either, although her car's in the driveway. I don't know where her head's at lately, but it hasn't been on the business."

He frowned. Steph was conscientious in all aspects of her well-ordered life. An unexplained absence wasn't like her. Cause for real concern here.

"She didn't give you any idea where she was going?"

"No, like I said, she was real secretive." Kat looked at Jessie, who slumped at the table holding the towel to her head. "You want I should get her some aspirin?"

"Please."

She went away to the kitchen, and Joseph asked Tony for a beer, then sat down opposite Jessie. His mind was still on Steph, but he said, "You sure you don't need medical attention? There's a twenty-four-hour emergency clinic at the Landing."

"No, I'm okay, really. More than anything else, I'm embarrassed."

"You ready to tell me why you were driving around up there?"

He listened as she described the conversation she'd had with Neil Woodsman at the Oceansong and how she'd followed him up the road toward the rez.

"Playing detective, were you?"

"Yeah. And I guess I'm not very good at it. I think he spotted me on the highway and led me up that road to lose me, then doubled back. My bad luck I'd started my turn when he came flying around the curve."

"You're saying it was Woodsman driving that car?"

"What I saw of it looked like his."

"He deliberately try to run you off the road?"

"No, that was my fault. I panicked. It was just a really weird accident, but Fitch is gonna kill me anyway."

"What *is* it with you and Fitch?"

"A bad professional pairing, although I'm starting to like him better. He's got his good points."

"If you say so."

Kat reappeared with the promised aspirin, deposited them in Jessie's hand, and retreated to the kitchen. Joseph drummed his fingers on the table, thinking again of Steph, while Jessie swallowed the tablets. He asked, "You said Gregory Erickson has gone to Sacramento?"

"That's what Woodsman told me. Something about fixing a problem with the paperwork they submitted to the water board."

"Late to be amending the apps, this close to the hearing."

"Well, I don't know. That's what he said." Jessie leaned her head on her hand, looking sick.

"You sure you're okay? You could have a concussion."

"I'm okay! All right?"

"Sorry."

"Look, I didn't mean to snap at you. I'm tired and I haven't eaten, and I think I need to get some takeout and go back to the motel."

"Arletta can box you up some of her fish-and-chips."

"That'd be great."

Joseph went to the kitchen and, finding Arletta busy, boxed them up himself. He offered to walk Jessie back to her room, but she declined and left, walking stiffly.

A tough woman, he thought. Bound and determined to have things her way, and maybe a little foolhardy because she was on unfamiliar territory, dealing with forces she — and he, for that matter — didn't understand. Foolhardy and stubborn and brave — a lot like the woman who had been the love of his life, and who now had gone missing.

Steph Pace

Steph couldn't shake the feeling she was being followed. She stopped walking, looked around, saw nothing but the rolling fog. Heard nothing, either. Of course, fog had the property of muting sound, as did the sandy ground beneath her feet. After a moment she went on, but the feeling was stronger than before.

Ahead, blurred by the mist, lay the jagged tumbledown cliffs that looked like a slumbering dinosaur. When she'd called Curtis to ask that he meet her, the beach at Cauldron Creek had immediately come to mind because, like the rhododendron grove, it would be deserted and they could talk privately. All she'd had to say was "where we spoke the other night," and he'd known what she meant, and agreed to be there in thirty minutes.

Strange that she didn't fear Curtis as she did Timothy McNear, even though she'd begun to suspect he had killed Mack.

An indistinct sound came from behind her. She whirled, saw only the fog. Why in

God's name had she insisted on such secrecy? Wouldn't it have been better if she and Curt had met in a crowded, well-lighted place like the Deluxe?

Well, no. You didn't talk about betrayal and murder in a crowd, or under revealing light. Better to have isolation and darkness. Besides, McNear had given her till the morning to find out if Curt was the waterbaggers' eyewitness, but she didn't trust him not to follow her and interfere. The beach was insurance against that; a man his age would never climb fog-blind down the steep trail. Steph, on the other hand, was agile and could have followed the trail in her sleep.

Another sound, louder. "Curt?" she called out.

No answer. No more sounds, either.

An animal. A deer or a stray dog. Probably as scared of me as I am of it.

She kept going.

How long had it been since her call to Curt? Thirty minutes, anyway. More like forty. Was he lurking in the fog, playing games with her?

She reached the sleeping dinosaur, leaned against its cold, damp flank. Realized she was panting — not from exertion but from fear. She got her breath more or less under control, peered up at the ledge where Curt had been sitting on Friday night. It was empty now.

He's late, that's all. Never been on time for anything in his life. No need to panic.

She was starting to relax some when the heavy weight dropped from the rocks above and smashed her to the ground.

Timothy McNear

Timothy walked along the path in his garden, tracing the route Stephanie Pace would have taken that night in 1984. It was very late — perhaps midnight, he wasn't sure — and an odd, stationary fog cloaked the tall palms.

Yes, this was the way Miss Stephanie would have come, past the statue of Kwan Yin. Stopped by the wall when she heard the shot. Then climbed over it, clutching the bag full of his money.

He hadn't asked her what they'd done with the cash. Three thousand dollars — not enough to care about. The money had never been important.

He turned, retraced his steps. The stones were moss-slick under his shoes, and he moved with care. Kwan Yin was crumbling; there was a chip on her nose. Dried fronds drifted against the trees' boles, and some of the flagstones were broken. He didn't often come into the garden, hadn't for years, and hadn't realized that the part-time groundskeeper had let it get so shabby. Caroline would have been horrified to see it in such a state, after all her efforts.

Doesn't matter now. None of those things do.

He reached the spot where Mack Kudge's body had lain. He'd known the boy by sight, had seen him hanging around the general store on the highway with Stephanie and her other friends. He'd never approved of any of them — wild, crude small-town kids who didn't seem worthy of her company — but who was he to speak out? Well, Kudge had come to the expected bad end — a worse end than he deserved.

He pictured the shocking stillness of the boy's body as he lay facedown, bleeding on the flagstones. Heard the moan that had risen in his own throat. Felt the suspicion that grew within him once his horror had passed. And the resolve that hardened after his suspicion was confirmed.

Not here, not in my garden, he'd thought. I can't let this happen to one of mine.

He still couldn't.

Timothy turned away from the garden, and from his memories.

Tuesday, February 24

Jessie Domingo

Jessie still had one hell of a headache, and Fitch wasn't helping it any. She sat at the little table in his motel room, clutching one of the cups of coffee that she'd brought along by way of apology for putting their rental car in the ditch, and listened to him rant.

"Jesus, every time I get to trusting you a little, you go and do something stupid! Chasing around in the middle of the night —"

"It wasn't the middle of the night."

"— after God knows what. It's irresponsible, and now we don't even have a car —"

"Joseph recommended a garage that'll tow it to the rental company in the Landing. They'll give us a new one."

"All at great cost, no doubt. And Joseph — what was he doing there?"

"Rescuing me, among other things."

"Your knight in shining armor."

"Well, you weren't around. *You* were probably talking to some friend's answering machine."

Fitch bit his lip and looked away.

"Listen, I shouldn't've said that."

"I didn't tell you those things so you could throw them back at me." He was hurt; she could see it in his eyes.

"I'm sorry."

"Yeah, well, so am I. That I ever said anything. So what do we have to do before we call the tow truck?"

Relieved that he wasn't going to harp on her careless remark, she got down to business. "One of us should notify the foundation's board members about Eldon."

"How about if we split the list?"

"Fine. We also need to go to the sheriff's department to give those statements Detective Swift wants. We could hitch a ride down there with the tow truck if the car's not driveable, bring the replacement back later. Maybe by now they've got some idea of what happened to Eldon."

"They'd've called if they knew anything."

"True. You know what I'm wondering? Those reports on Erickson and Woodsman that the detective mentioned in his e-mail to Eldon — did he ever receive them? And if so, where are they now?"

"I'd forgotten about them. They were coming by courier, right?"

"Right. I'll phone the Tides. Someone there'll probably remember if they arrived."

But no one at Eldon's motel could recall a special delivery from San Francisco.

"Doesn't mean anything," Fitch told her. "The person who accepted the package could be off duty. Check back later."

"What about calling the private investigator? What's his name? Tom Little? You've had dealings with him."

"Right. I'll give him a ring."

Tom Little was out of the office and not expected back till afternoon. As Fitch hung up the receiver, he looked at his watch. "Nine here, noon at home. I don't know about you, but that gives me the perfect excuse to delay calling the board members."

When Jessie phoned the garage Joseph had recommended, the tow truck driver agreed to pick them up at the motel, pull the rental car from the ditch, and give them a ride to Calvert's Landing, if necessary. "But you never know — your vehicle may be in better shape than you think," he added cheerfully.

And it was: a number of scratches and a dent on the right front quarter panel, but perfectly driveable. Fitch, who had usurped the keys before they left the motel, muttered for miles about not knowing how they were going to explain to the foundation about the extra charges for the damage, and Jessie was tempted to tell him to shut up, but his grousing was really very mild compared to his earlier tirade, so she let him vent. After a while he seemed to get tired of the sound of his own voice.

The substation on Center Street looked brand-new — which it was, Rhoda Swift explained as she led them to her office, the headquarters for coastal law enforcement having been moved north from less populous Signal Port six months before. Swift's work space was small but comfortable, with beige walls and dark-brown carpeting and windows that overlooked a courtyard with picnic benches. Diplomas and citations and a photograph of a goofy-looking Labrador retriever hung on the walls, and a studio portrait of an attractive man with silvery hair and a craggy face sat on the desk. While Fitch waited outside, Swift taped Jessie's statement, then began asking questions.

"Does Mr. Whitesides usually involve himself personally in the cases his employees are pursuing?"

"Not usually, no. But he took a special interest in Cape Perdido."

"Why?"

"I guess because it will set important precedent if our side prevails."

"What did he plan to do here?"

". . . I guess he wanted to be on hand to make sure nothing went wrong. To advise Mr. Collier and me, you know."

"And he needed to travel all that way to give advice?"

What was Swift getting at? "I guess he felt he did."

"You seem to be guessing at quite a few things, Ms. Domingo."

Everything about Swift — her business-like tone, her direct way of meeting one's eye, even her well-tailored woolen blazer — was making Jessie feel nervous and unsure of herself. She stifled the words, "I guess I am," and instead said, "Mr. Whitesides didn't confide in me. I'm a relatively new employee, and I wasn't his first choice for this assignment."

Swift made a couple of notes on a legal pad in front of her. "Tell me, Ms. Domingo, does Mr. Whitesides have any connections with anyone in the immediate area?"

Joseph's relationship to Eldon — Swift had seen the stuff about him on Eldon's computer.

"He and Joseph Openshaw went to college together."

"And how would you characterize their relationship?"

"I . . . don't think they like each other very much."

"Why not?"

Jessie stifled another "I guess." "They're coming from different places. Opposite places, really."

"A philosophical difference?"

"More one of style. Joseph's an old-type ecologist — very Berkeley, if you know what I mean. Eldon's more into the big money."

"I see. Would you say that in spite of their differences they get along?"

"Well enough. They certainly agree on stopping the waterbaggers from destroying the Perdido."

"Any arguments between them since Mr. Whitesides has been here?"

"None that I know of." Joseph's prickliness over Eldon's use of the private investigator didn't constitute an argument.

"Did Joseph Openshaw know where Mr. Whitesides was staying?"

"I don't know. You'd have to ask him."

"I intend to." Swift switched off the tape recorder and stood. "We'll be in touch when we have further information, Ms. Domingo. If you'd ask Mr. Collier to come in . . . ?"

"Certainly." Jessie moved toward the door.

"And, Ms. Domingo, I hear your dad was one hell of a ballplayer."

She turned, surprised.

Swift grinned. "My significant other is a New Yorker, and a Mets fan. I've heard all about Kip Domingo."

Now, why would Swift have been talking to her boyfriend about Dad? The answer was obvious: she'd been gathering background information on her. Did she consider her a suspect in Eldon's disappearance?

Joseph Openshaw

Joseph had been to half a dozen places looking for Curtis when he finally spotted him, patching the roof of the general store. He pulled his van onto the shoulder, jogged across the highway, and hollered for him to come down.

"No time," Curt called. "I got another job this afternoon."

Business must be booming for Curt to have two jobs in a week, let alone in a day. "Get your ass down here," Joseph insisted. "It's important."

Curt made a leisurely process of nailing another shingle in place before descending the ladder. Just being contrary, Joseph thought. If he'd told him to take his time, he'd've been down in two seconds.

"Okay, what is it?" Curt asked, wiping his hands on the front of his denim work shirt.

"Have you seen Steph?"

Something flickered in Curt's eyes. "Not for a couple of days. What's the matter, she hiding from you?"

"She left the restaurant yesterday afternoon and never came back. I've checked her house and everyplace else I can think of. There's no sign of her, but her car's in her driveway."

"So why d'you think I'd know where she is?"

"Last resort."

"Well, you're outta luck." Curt turned back toward his ladder.

Joseph had known him too long to miss the subtle changes in his posture and tone that indicated he was hiding something. "You sure you haven't seen or heard from her?"

"Do I have to say it twice?"

"Dammit, I'm really worried, and you should be, too. This isn't like Steph."

Curt whirled on him, scowling. "Look, Joseph, why don't you lay off Steph? She's a grown woman; she doesn't have to answer to you. You want things to be different, you should do something about it."

"What's that supposed to mean?"

"Years ago, you walked out on her. Now you're back in town, hanging around her restaurant every day but still pretending it's all over. You want her close but not too close, but you can't have it both ways. Either make a commitment or cut her loose."

Joseph stared at Curt as he started up the ladder, restraining an urge to drag him down and have it out once and for all. His former friend was right about his treatment of Steph, but that didn't change the fact that he was withholding something important.

Joseph went by Steph's house again and found it as empty as before. He debated stopping in at the restaurant, then decided to go home and call rather than face the staff's growing anxiety in person. For some reason they looked to him for advice on what to do. They were running low on produce; a delivery hadn't arrived; the receipts from the day before hadn't been deposited. Well, what was he supposed to tell them? Just because he ate there frequently and had coffee in the bar every afternoon didn't mean he knew how to run the damn place.

When he let himself into the shed, the light on his answering machine was blinking. Two calls.

Detective Rhoda Swift of the SCSD: "You may have heard that Eldon Whitesides of Environmental Consultants Clearinghouse is missing. I'd like to set up an appointment to talk with you about him. I understand the two of you have known each other a long time, and any insights you can provide may be helpful."

So that particular shit was about to hit the fan.

Ike Kudge: "Hey, Joseph. I asked around about Whitesides for you, and I've got something interesting. I'm meeting some guys at the Deluxe around noon, and if you want, we can talk beforehand."

Joseph looked at his watch. Nearly eleven o'clock. He'd call the restaurant in case Steph had put in an appearance, then go see what Kudge had to tell him.

Steph Pace

The place was cold and dark. Small, too. Rough board walls, and Steph had splinters from beating her fists on them. Faint light shone under what she assumed was a door, but not enough to tell her what sort of structure this might be. It was isolated; that much she knew — she'd screamed herself hoarse, and no one had come to help her.

She remembered nothing of being brought here, had awakened from a heavy unconsciousness and found she was lying on her side, face pillowed on her elbow. Her limbs were cramped, and she had a bloody scrape on her cheek. There were painful spots on her back that must be bruises. Nothing broken, apparently, although she had a headache and was sick to her stomach. She lay still, trying to control the queasiness. After a while she felt better.

When she was able to move, she sat up and began exploring the space with her hands. They encountered nothing but four walls and a concrete floor. She got to her feet. The light was coming from beneath a door, tightly fitted in its frame. The knob wouldn't turn. She got down on her knees and put her eye to the crack beneath it. All she could make out was hard-packed earth and tufts of grass.

That was when she panicked. She'd pried at the door, then pounded on it and the walls. Screamed and kicked, too. Damn near exhausted herself, and now she lay on the floor again.

How in hell had this happened to her? The last things she remembered were the beach and the feeling of being followed, the sounds in the fog, then someone jumping off the rocks and knocking the breath out of her. After that . . .

No recollection.

The way she felt reminded her of when she'd come out of the general anesthesia after she'd had her gallbladder removed. The inside of her right elbow was tender; she fingered it, found what felt like a puncture wound. That meant that whoever jumped her had immediately drugged her. Then brought her to this place and left her, perhaps to die.

Don't think like that.

The quality of light seeping under the door had changed. Natural light, shifting as the sun moved. From its intensity she guessed it was midday. The air around her was warming. If the temperature climbed as much as yesterday's forecast had predicted, it would get so hot in here that she might suffocate.

Fear spread through her, making her arms and legs go weak. She could hear her pulse pound. She had to pee, and fought the urge, concentrating instead on her other senses.

I see . . . nothing but the seeping sunlight.

I smell . . . old wood and damp earth. Mold. And a faint smokiness . . . charred wood. Am I at the mill? No, the smell's not strong enough. But I'm near it, at least close enough for wind to carry the fire residue.

I hear . . . humming. Distant. Gets louder, then softer, sometimes stops altogether. What's that? A truck downshifting. Big one, maybe a logging rig. The highway. But it's a good ways off.

Where?

And who?

And why?

Just going to leave me here, or will they come back for me? I must've been missed by now. Arletta, Tony, Kim, and Kat. Joseph.

Curtis — what happened to Curtis? He didn't do this to me, did he?

Timothy McNear . . . I promised I'd call him after I talked with Curt. He'll know something's gone wrong, but will he do anything about it?

Arletta, Tony, Kim, Kat.

Joseph.

Somebody, please.

Timothy McNear

Miss Stephanie hadn't called. He'd waited till well after midnight, then gone to bed but slept little, listening for the phone. This morning the housekeeper had arrived early, and the noise of her vacuum cleaner and floor waxer threatened to drive him insane. He kept checking the light on the answering machine, afraid he hadn't heard the bell. Who *could* hear — much less think — with such goings-on?

At eleven-thirty he gave up waiting and drove to town. The fog had lifted, and the calm, blue sea stretched before him as he came down the hill. His whole life, with the exception of his four years at Stanford, he'd lived beside it, but he'd never become indifferent to its beauty. Today, distracted as he was, he barely gave it notice.

Stephanie Pace lived on Hill Street, in the little house where she'd been raised, alone now, since her mother had gone to a retirement community down in Westhaven. Timothy parked in the driveway behind Miss Stephanie's blue station wagon, went up on the porch, and knocked at the door. No response.

Of course — it was lunchtime. By now she'd be at the restaurant. He got back into his car and drove to the Blue Moon.

She wasn't there, either.

Outside, Timothy stood indecisively by the door. A couple of men brushed past him, eyeing him with startled recognition. Soon word would be out that the ogre had come to town, and what then? Would he be shunned? Verbally assaulted?

Not wishing to find out, he got back in his car and drove to the deserted scenic overlook north of the volunteer fire department. Parked there and thought.

Where was Miss Stephanie? Where had she gone after they talked at the rhododendron preserve? Home, surely, because her car was in the driveway. She had probably called Curtis Hope. But then . . . ?

The man he'd spoken with at the restaurant had seemed nervous when Timothy asked for her. Not the type of behavior he'd expect from an employee if she had simply taken the day off. Something wrong, then.

What?

Curtis Hope, he thought. That's what.

Jessie Domingo

"Yes, sir, I'll let you know if the sheriff's department finds out anything." Jessie replaced the receiver and sighed deeply. Her share of the calls to the foundation's board members was completed. Now what?

A knock at the door. Fitch. She called out, and he entered, frowning. "I just got off the phone with an official at the state water resources control board," he said. "One of the foundation's directors asked me to call there, explain the situation, ask for a postponement on the hearing."

"Did they agree?"

"They'll consider it. But here's the thing that interests me: those two employees of Gregory Erickson's came into the state offices this morning to amend the apps, but he wasn't with them."

"Maybe he sent them to do the scut work while he played tourist, or whatever guys like him do. Or maybe he's not in Sacramento like Woodsman claimed. And if he's not, where is he?"

Fitch shrugged.

"Okay, for the sake of argument, let's say Erickson didn't go to Sacramento. But he did check out of his motel room. Why?"

"He went to attend to some other project? Or went back to their headquarters in North Carolina? I wouldn't think he'd do either, with the hearings so close."

"One way to find out." Jessie took the thin coastal directory from the nightstand, looked up the number of the small airport at Oilville. Yes, the woman who answered told her, a chartered plane had picked up a party of two bound for Sacramento the previous afternoon.

"Only two? Did you happen to catch their names?"

"Sorry, I didn't."

"Was one of them tall and slender, with prominent teeth and a receding hairline? Spoke with a southern accent?"

"No. These guys were southern, but one was short and fat, and they both had a lot of hair."

"Has the other man I described flown anywhere else?"

"No other charters have gone out in the past twenty-four hours."

Jessie thanked her and hung up the receiver. "Erickson didn't go to Sacramento — or fly anywhere."

"So he drove. Where?"

"San Francisco Airport, and then North Carolina?"

"Check it out."

Jessie looked up the number of Aqueduct Systems' home office in her file. Erickson's secretary said he was in California and gave the number of the Shorebird.

Jessie replaced the receiver. "They think he's still here."

"Well, he's not, and Woodsman lied about his whereabouts."

"Maybe he really thought Erickson went to Sacramento with the others. There must be some way I can find out."

Fitch looked alarmed. "Jessie, you're not going to do something stupid again?"

"No, I'm not going to do something stupid!" Then she grinned. "Maybe this time I'll think of something clever."

Joseph Openshaw

Ike Kudge was holding court at one of the pool tables when Joseph got to the Deluxe. He leaned on his cue, beer gut hanging over his belt, haranguing two skinny guys in deliverymen's uniforms who looked as though they just wanted to be left alone to play pool. Something to do with the San Francisco Forty Niners' dismal prospects for the upcoming season. When he saw Joseph, he racked his cue, went to a nearby table where a half-full mug of beer sat, and motioned him over.

"You want a beer?" Ike asked. "I'll buy."

"A little early for me."

"Still the good, clean-living boy, huh?"

"Not hardly. So what've you got?"

"What, no 'How are you, Ike'? No small talk?"

God, why was he cursed with contrary people today? He was in no mood for this shit. "How are you, Ike?" he said.

"That's better. Now we can get down to business." Ike leaned forward on his elbows; the table creaked under his weight. "I talked with a couple guys I know from the Landing, somebody down at the Westhaven, too. There's no word out about your Mr. Whitesides."

"And that's it? You asked me here to tell me nothing?"

Ike leaned back in his chair, smiling and sipping beer. "Getting pretty testy for a man wants a favor."

"Look, Ike, this is serious. Whitesides isn't the only person who's gone missing."

"Oh? Who else?"

"Steph Pace."

"Your old girlfriend, the Blue Moon lady?"

"That's right."

"Since when?"

"Late yesterday afternoon. Any word out on that?"

"There won't be, not yet. Been my experience that you need about twenty-four hours before something gets on the grapevine."

"Will you keep listening?"

"For Steph's sake, yes. I like her, even if she does have bad taste in men. What is it with people disappearing, anyway?"

"Wish I knew."

Ike finished his beer, folded his hands on his stomach, and regarded Joseph thoughtfully. "How come both missing people've got something to do with you?"

"Whitesides is only connected with me through the Friends of the Perdido."

"But Steph — the two of you go way back. She a member of the Friends?"

"Nominally, but she's not active in the organization. The restaurant takes up all her time. Why d'you ask?"

"What I heard. Has to do with that water bag."

"So you *did* hear something. What?"

"Getting testy again. Watch it."

"Don't play games with me, Ike."

"You always was a scrapper, no matter if the other guy was twice your size. Beat the crap out of me that time I stole your dope stash. Don't you think I ever forgave you for that, either." Ike glared at him for a moment, then said, "Okay, what I heard is a guy called Wes Landis took out that bag. Lives on the ridge near Deer Harbor, kind of a survivalist and small-time thief. Year or two ago, he stole a rifle outta Curt Hope's truck, and that was what he used."

"Why?"

"Couldn't be traced to him."

"No, why did this Wes shoot up the bag? What was in it for him?"

"Money, of course. Somebody paid him

five hundred bucks for the job."

"Who?"

Ike grinned slowly, rocked his chair back. "And you thought I asked you here to tell you nothin'."

Joseph concealed his impatience, meeting his gaze steadily. After a moment Ike's grin faded and he let the chair's legs drop to the floor.

"Okay," he said, "I don't know a name, but I can tell you where to find Landis."

Wes Landis lived in a trailer in a cluttered clearing in the woods east of Deer Harbor. As Joseph drove in on a dirt track from Dry Creek Road, he counted a Jeep, two motorcycles, a pickup, a tractor, and a dump truck. Ike Kudge had said Landis lived alone; what in God's name did one man do with so much motorized equipment?

Joseph got out of his van and followed the sound of a chain saw into the trees, where he found a tall, balding man in army fatigues working on a thick stump. The man couldn't hear him approach, and when he spotted him out of the corner of his protective goggles, he started. Then he shut off the saw and held it as if it were a weapon.

"Wes Landis?" Joseph said.

"Yeah, whadda you want?"

"I'm Joseph Openshaw. Ike Kudge told me where to find you."

Landis's mouth twisted. "That asshole? I don't deal with him, no way."

"Why not?"

"Because he cooks meth, man. If you're one of his druggie friends, you better get off my property." He took a step forward, raising the chain saw higher.

Joseph held up his hands. "Kudge is no friend of mine; he just gave me directions to you. I've got a business proposition."

Suspicious narrowing of the eyes, as well as a glint of greed. "What kind of proposition?"

"A hundred bucks for information."

"About what?"

"About who approached you to shoot up the water bag at the mill last weekend."

Landis's hands tightened on the saw. "I don't know nothin' about no water bag."

"This information is strictly for myself. It goes no farther." Joseph took out his wallet, counted five twenties, folded them. Landis watched him, running his tongue over his lips.

"I didn't shoot that bag," he said.

"Don't claim you did. But somebody approached you. Who?"

"You lay that money down on that other stump there. Then step back some, and we'll talk."

Joseph set the bills where he indicated, and moved away.

"Okay," Landis said, "this woman came up here. Said one of the guys works at the feed store was talking about somebody should take that bag out, and that I was the man for the job."

"Why would he think that?"

"Because I'm a good shot, man. I won medals in competitions five years running. Anyway, I sent her packing. I don't do shit like that."

You do, and you did, but it doesn't matter.

"This woman have a name?"

"She didn't give it, but I seen her around. She runs that Friends of the Perdido group."

That was the last thing he'd expected to hear. It was a moment before he could ask, "Bernina Tobin?"

"I don't know, man. Like I say, she didn't tell me who she was, and I didn't shoot that bag. You better not try to say I did."

"I'm not going to say a word. But you already have — to too many people for your own good."

"Listen, I didn't do it!"

"Then stop talking about it." Joseph turned and went back to his van.

Goddamn Bernina, he thought, fumbling with the keys with fingers made unsteady by rage. She may have undone everything we've worked so hard for.

Steph Pace

The temperature in the cramped space was climbing steadily. With every degree Steph felt more light-headed, thirsty, and once again sick to her stomach. On a shelf she'd located a few items: a bag of something that felt like hardened cement, a ball of twine, an empty plastic spray bottle, a bucket, a trowel. She used the bucket for a toilet, the trowel to pry around the door.

After a protracted effort that produced only splinters, she gave up and lay back on the floor. When would the day's heat wane? She had lost all sense of time, and the shaft of light had disappeared from under the door, but the heat continued unabated. Whatever this building was, it must be shaded on the east side, exposed on the west.

Already today she'd missed two meal services at the restaurant. She lived her life on a strict schedule; her employees must be frantic. Had they gone to her house? Searched elsewhere for her? Called her friends and her mother? If so, had they then contacted the sheriff's department? Would the department put deputies on the lookout for her, notify the highway patrol? They did that in cases of people who were driving the remote county roads and didn't arrive at their destinations within a reasonable time, but Steph's car was parked in her own driveway. She hadn't wanted it to attract attention at Cauldron Creek last night, so she'd walked. The authorities might argue that her absence appeared to be voluntary.

But Joseph would realize she hadn't gone off of her own free will. He knew her, perhaps better than she knew herself. Joseph would have stopped by the restaurant for his afternoon coffee by now; he would be looking for her, even if the sheriff's deputies weren't.

Joseph.

He'd find her.

He would.

Timothy McNear

When he'd driven by on his way to Miss
Stephanie's house, Timothy had seen Curtis
Hope replacing shingles on the roof of the
general store. Now he drove back down
there, but Hope was gone. He parked and
went inside, asked the clerk behind the
counter if Hope would return. No, she told
him, the repairs were done and he'd left for
another job. Where? Timothy asked. The
clerk popped her chewing gum and eyed him
suspiciously, then said it was one of the
houses off Lone Pine Trail, the old Adams
place.

Timothy knew the house; it had been
abandoned for years since the deaths of the
couple who owned it, and he was surprised
someone had hired Hope to fix it up. The
son, returned from the Los Angeles area,
or perhaps a new owner? He went back to
his car and drove south.

Hope, he thought. Hope must be behind
Stephanie's absence. Whatever he'd done
to her, he certainly was acting cool, going
about his business where everyone could

see him. Unusual behavior for a man with something to hide, but hadn't he himself done the same after he'd moved Mack Kudge's body those many years ago?

The morning after that far-off night, he'd arrived at the mill offices at his accustomed hour of eight. Greeted his secretary, read the San Francisco, Sacramento, and Santa Carla papers at his desk, sipping the coffee she brought him. As he signed a stack of letters he'd dictated the previous afternoon, his hand did not waver. Outwardly calm, even relaxed, but his thoughts were in a turmoil.

How soon before someone discovered Kudge's body? The workers often took smoke or lunch breaks on the long-unused pier. Perhaps it would have been wiser to dump the body into the sea, let it wash up somewhere south of here. But he'd thought it a clever move to leave it at the mill; no one would be stupid enough to dump a dead body on his own property.

Ten o'clock, and still no alarm had been sounded. He indulged in a fantasy that the events of the previous night had been nothing more than a bad dream. Then the present became part of the nightmare: What if someone had seen him move the body? Notified the sheriff's department?

Perhaps they were playing a game with him, waiting for him to go to the pier to see if the body was still there.

Were the sheriff's deputies really that cunning? he wondered. No, not the clownish bunch at the coastal substation. Underqualified, inept, shunted off into this backwater because serious crime didn't happen much here and the department needed its better people in the cities along the inland corridor.

Still, he had refused to give in to the urge to go to the pier, have a look.

It was after eleven when his secretary burst through the door with the news. Timothy rushed to the pier, viewed the body in the presence of his head of security and the workers who had found it. He didn't have to feign shock and queasiness; even though Kudge's remains had been sheltered from the sun by a stack of old packing crates, the morning heat had done them no good, and daylight revealed details that darkness had softened. Blood had flowed from Kudge's mouth and nostrils, drying brown on his face. Flies hovered around the body, and already the smell of putrefaction was on the air. He turned away.

So much destruction in so little time. A brief

hesitation, a squeeze of the trigger, and . . . this.

Or had there been a hesitation? Was the fatal shot more calculated than he'd imagined? And if so, how was he to live with that knowledge? He'd pushed the unwelcome thought away and gone to speak with his security man.

Now, as he drove south in search of Curtis Hope, the same thought returned, and he had to push it away even more firmly. Entertaining it, even for a minute, would force him to examine the validity of his actions of twenty years ago, and he doubted he could go on if he concluded that what he'd considered a great and noble sacrifice had been based on a dangerously false premise. Dangerous because of what further acts of violence that sacrifice might have spawned.

Lone Pine Trail wound eastward into the hills above the wide spot in the highway called Deer Harbor. Timothy followed it for half a mile or so to a gravel driveway where a rusted mailbox leaned on its post, the door gaping open. The rambling white clapboard house was on a rise, a meadow that was green from recent rains, sloping down to the roadside. When he turned in, he saw an old white pickup under an acacia tree. He parked beside it and walked toward the house.

Curtis Hope sat in an old swing on the wide wraparound porch, smoking a cigarette. He stood when he saw Timothy, crushed the butt out under his toe, and folded his arms across his barrel chest. Timothy went to the foot of the steps and stopped.

"Mr. Hope." He nodded. "The clerk at the general store told me I might find you here."

"Yeah? So what can I do for you?"

"I'm looking for a mutual friend, Stephanie Pace."

Something changed in Hope's face, a tightening of its already taut lines. "Stephanie isn't really a friend of mine. Surprises me that you count her as one of yours."

"As I recall, you used to be close to her."

"That was years ago. Things change. People change."

Timothy hesitated. He hadn't thought through his approach to Hope, and now he didn't know the best way to counter this resistance.

Hope saved him the effort. "Look, man," he said, "I don't know why everybody thinks I know where Steph is. I haven't seen her in days."

"What do you mean, everybody?"

"Well, Joseph Openshaw. He was asking about her earlier. I told him the same thing: I haven't seen her since the Friends of the Perdido dinner on Friday night."

Hope took out another cigarette and got it lit, but his hand shook. Timothy studied him, taking his time the way he used to during labor negotiations at the mill. Hope had been an outstanding student, reputedly destined for far better things than Soledad County could offer, but now he was simply another underemployed victim of the poor economy and his own laziness.

A victim of his guilt, too. The man was gradually being eaten up by it. Guilt that could be traced directly back to that night in June 1984. A man with a core of guilt could easily be broken. Timothy knew that better than anyone.

He said, "I know Stephanie wanted to talk with you last night. Did she tell you why?"

Hope's mouth tightened; then he dragged on the cigarette. "I told you, I haven't seen her since Friday night."

"But you heard from her."

". . . What if I did? It's none of your business."

"But it is. You see, I asked her to talk

with you. About Mack Kudge."

Hope flinched at the name. "Kudge? That was decades ago."

"And decades are a long time to keep a secret. I know; I have a few of my own."

"Man, you're crazy!"

"Secrets like ours can make you crazy. Don't you agree?"

Hope was silent, his lips compressed, his eyes moving jerkily from side to side, as if he were looking for a way out of a trap. "I'm not gonna talk about Kudge. Not to you, not to anybody."

"But you did agree to talk with Stephanie."

"I didn't know what she wanted. If I'd've known, I never would've —"

"Yes?"

"Look, all she said was that she wanted to talk. Named a time and place."

"When and where?"

Hope looked away.

"When and where?"

"Eight o'clock. The beach at Cauldron Creek."

"Did you meet her?"

"No."

"Why not?"

"She didn't show."

"Are you sure of that?"

"Well, no, I'm not sure. I mean, I was late, my truck wouldn't start, and . . ."

"And what?"

Hope ran his tongue over his lips, then nodded as if making a decision. "Okay, when I got there, it looked like somebody'd gotten to her first. The sand was all scuffed up like there'd been some kind of fight, and on the rocks, well, there was a smear of blood."

Timothy felt anger constrict his throat. It was a moment before he could speak, and when he did, his voice was low and dangerous — the tone that had often made the union leaders back off during negotiations. "You saw signs of a struggle, you saw blood, and yet you did nothing?"

Hope glared at him. "Yeah, I did nothing. I've been doing nothing my whole life. Nothing, ever since that night somebody shot Mack Kudge dead in your goddamn garden."

Jessie Domingo

Jessie waved at Fitch as the small plane sped down the runway of the airport near Oilville. It rose into the air, cleared the trees at the far end, and soon was gone, turning southeast toward Sacramento. They'd both agreed he could do more there, monitoring developments with the water resources control board, than in Cape Perdido.

She got back into the battered rental car, drove along the access road to the highway, and turned south, feeling aimless and adrift. Before she and Fitch had left the motel, he'd called Tom Little, the private investigator in San Francisco; again Little wasn't available, but his secretary promised to ask him to call back. Then Jessie called the sheriff's department. Rhoda Swift wasn't available, either, so she left a message. Now all she could do was go to her shabby motel room and wait to hear from one or the other.

The room was much too quiet; even the rumble of the logging trucks on the highway was muted. For a while Jessie tried to read, but the novel she'd brought along — a multigenerational saga set in South Africa, the sort of thing she usually liked — seemed tedious and impenetrable. Finally she set it aside and lay flat on the bed, staring at the cracked ceiling.

Inactivity had never suited her. At home her days were packed with work, visits to the health club, classes, lunch dates, dinner parties, clubbing, plays, movies, trips to the museums, weekend excursions out of town. Even her downtime couldn't really be called that; there were always errands to run, friends to talk with, plans to be made. Sometimes she feared that she was leading an uncontemplative life, but mostly she was content. As her Puerto Rican grandmother had once told her, later there would be plenty of time to contemplate, but not so much to live fully.

What she was not content with right now was waiting for a call from Swift or Little that might not come. She sat up, reached for the phone directory, and found the number for the Tides Inn. Called and asked the man who answered if he'd been on the desk the night before. He had, he said, two in the afternoon till ten in the evening. Did he recall a courier bringing a package for Mr. Eldon Whitesides? she asked.

A pause. "That's the guest who's missing."

"Right."

"Are you with the sheriff's department?"

"No, I work for Mr. Whitesides."

"I don't know if I should be talking —"

"I'm assisting Detective Rhoda Swift with the investigation." More or less.

"Oh, well, an envelope came by AeroCouriers at around nine-thirty. I signed for it."

"Did you take it to his room, or did he come down for it?"

"Neither. His guest delivered it."

"Guest? Who was that?"

"I don't know her name. She came in while I was signing for the package. Asked for his room number, and said she'd take the package to him. I probably shouldn't've given it to her, but I was alone on the desk and it's inn policy never to leave it unmanned."

"Did you tell anyone from the sheriff's department about this woman or the package?"

"Not yet. The manager said somebody would be around to interview me later."

"Can you describe the woman for me?"

"Dark-haired, short, kind of heavy. Maybe thirty-five. She was dressed real retro — long flowered skirt, green velvet cape. Talked different, like maybe she wasn't from around here."

Bernina Tobin, with her flowing clothes and Maine accent.

Bernina was home and welcomed Jessie into her cozy parlor. Rag rugs dotted the hardwood floor, and chintz-covered furnishings that looked more New England than Pacific Coast crowded the smallish space. She said she'd make tea, brushed aside Jessie's protests, and went away to the kitchen, trailing a lavender scent that reminded Jessie of her third-grade teacher. Even at home Bernina dressed with her somewhat odd flair, today in an embroidered Chinese tunic and wide-legged jeans.

She returned with a tray holding two steaming mugs and a plate of carrot cake, urged Jessie to help herself. Then she took her own mug to the sofa and sat with her legs drawn up beneath her. "I'm glad you stopped by," she said. "I wondered what happened to you when you didn't return my call yesterday, and when I heard Eldon Whitesides is missing . . . well, I got really freaked. Didn't you get my messages?"

She had, but she'd set them aside. "They're not terribly efficient with messages at the Shorebird. I've been meaning to get in touch with you. I understand you went to see Eldon at the Tides Inn the night he disappeared."

Bernina frowned. "Who told you that?"

"The desk clerk."

"I see. Well, yes, I did."

"Why?"

"I wanted to talk about his strategy for stopping the waterbaggers."

"You couldn't talk about that in front of the rest of us?"

"Not really. I sensed you and Joseph didn't approve of his methods, and I thought I should assure him of my support."

"Support for digging up dirt on people and using it to coerce them?"

"You make it sound so . . . slimy."

"It *is* slimy."

"Jessie, how many situations like this one have you been involved in?"

"None."

"Then you don't know. Sometimes you have to resort to desperate measures in order to achieve your ends. Joseph realizes that, but he's still living in the old days, when desperate measures amounted to tying oneself to a tree when the loggers came to cut it down. Nowadays . . . well, you do what's necessary."

"So you offered your support to Eldon."

"Yes, and he was grateful. He said that a solution might be contained in the package I'd brought up to him, but that he'd have to study the documents and talk to some people before he'd know for sure. I left so he could do that. And now he's missing."

"What time did you leave?"

"I couldn't've been there more than half an hour. So ten o'clock, maybe. Jessie, what do you suppose was in those documents?"

"Information on the waterbaggers, I suppose."

"Who did he plan to talk with?"

There was a banging at the door.

Bernina glanced that way, her brow knitting. "Now, who . . . ?"

Joseph's voice called out, "Bernina! Open up."

"What's with him?" she muttered, unfolding her legs and getting to her feet.

"Bernina, I know you're in there!"

"Hold on, I'm coming."

But before she got to the door, it burst open, and Joseph stormed into the entryway, his face red with fury. "You goddamn idiot!" he exclaimed. "What the hell did you think you were doing, hiring a sniper?"

Joseph Openshaw

Bernina stood in front of him, her mouth flopping open and closed like a fish out of water. Her exaggerated look of innocence further enraged him, and while he had never struck a woman in his life, in the seconds before he saw Jessie Domingo rise from her seat in the parlor, he almost took a swing at Bernina.

He balled his fists at his sides, breathed deeply, got himself under control. Then he asked again, "What the hell were you thinking of?"

"I didn't —"

"Don't deny it to me. I tracked down the scumbag you hired. Cost me a hundred bucks, and he wouldn't actually admit to doing the job, but he confirmed that you approached him."

"What scumbag? I don't know who you're talking about."

Jessie had come to the archway leading into the parlor. "Joseph?" she said. "What's this about a sniper?"

"This one" — he flung out his arm at

Bernina — "hired a guy named Wes Landis to shoot up that water bag."

Jessie's eyes narrowed; she turned to Bernina. "Is that true?"

Bernina's defiant expression faded, and she backed up against the wall. "I was only trying to help our cause. I thought that if they saw how violently opposed we are —"

"Help?" Joseph exclaimed. "Do you realize what damage you may have done?"

"Nobody knows what I did but you two — and Landis."

"Plenty of people know. Landis couldn't keep his mouth shut, and it's being whispered about up and down the coast. Only a matter of time before the sheriff's department hears one of those whispers. I just hope it's after the state water board hearings; if you're arrested, it could tip them in favor of Aqueduct."

"Arrested?"

"That's what usually happens to people who hire someone to destroy property."

Bernina paled, put her fingertips to her lips. "You wouldn't . . . ?"

Joseph's anger suddenly left him; he felt spent both from it and from his growing concern for Steph. "No, I'm not going to the sheriff, if that's what you're thinking. That would discredit the Friends and destroy everything we've worked for. I'm hoping they're so focused on Eldon's disappearance and the fire at the mill that the water bag incident has become a minor issue."

Jessie cleared her throat. "Joseph, I think you should know that Bernina visited Eldon at his motel the night he disappeared."

Good God, would the unpleasant surprises never stop coming? "Why?"

Bernina said, "I wanted to tell him I supported his efforts, even if you didn't."

"Did you also tell him about hiring the sniper?"

"Yes. He congratulated me."

"Jesus! And then what? He decided to disappear and create an even bigger commotion?"

"No, no. It wasn't like that at all. I don't know why he disappeared, and I didn't have anything to do with it. You *have* to believe that."

"I don't have to believe anything you say." He closed his eyes for a moment, thinking. "Okay, here's what you're going to do: Get in your car and drive, I don't care where. San Francisco, farther south — anyplace so long as it's a long way from here. Make yourself unavailable till after the water board hearings."

"And then?"

"Then you resign from the Friends. Don't make a big deal out of it. Say you've been having health problems or something."

"But what will I do with myself? The Friends are all I have."

"Too bad. If I were you, I'd seriously consider moving away from here. Go back to Maine, wherever. What you did is going to come out, but the sheriff is less likely to pursue an investigation if you're history."

Bernina's mouth turned down, but she didn't protest, just bowed her head and moved away into the parlor.

Joseph said to Jessie, "Let's get the hell out of here."

Steph Pace

She must have passed out from the heat, because now she was lying on her back, enveloped in a refreshing coolness. The light under the door had turned a murky gray. Near evening, then, and still no one had come for her.

She got onto her knees, crawled to the door. Lay flat on her stomach, nose to the crack, and breathed deeply of fresh air scented with growing things and damp earth. Her mouth and the membranes of her nose were dry, her lips cracked. She was hungry and thirsty, and she tried not to think about food or water.

After a moment she pushed up and rocked back on her heels. The motion made her light-headed. She braced her palms on the floor beside her.

When the dizziness cleared, she got to her feet and began feeling around the walls again. Nothing but the shelf she'd discovered earlier. She moved her hands over it slowly but touched only the plastic spray bottle, twine, and the bag with its hardened contents. Down on her knees again, she began feeling along the bottom of the wall. There might be some gap in the foundation that she'd missed.

Halfway along the wall opposite the door, her fingers encountered a small object that was lodged between the board and the concrete. She pulled it out and felt it. Hard plastic, odd shape, with curves and ridges. Some kind of toy. Yes, a toy soldier. Like the ones Max and Shelby had marched across a make-believe battlefield . . .

Now she knew where she was: the old potting shed in Timothy McNear's garden.

Timothy McNear

The clerk at the Cape Perdido Chevron station told Timothy that Joseph Openshaw lived on Oceanside Drive. "There's a little yellow house with this funky outbuilding behind it. The outbuilding's his."

Until now, Timothy had never considered the advantages of living in a town where everyone knew everyone else and his business. Previously the enforced closeness had only presented drawbacks.

Oceanside Drive branched off the highway near the feed-and-surplus store and meandered uphill for about half a mile. The houses were all small, shingled or clapboard, and architecturally insignificant. A car was pulled up in front of the bright yellow house, and a woman was loading suitcases into it. Timothy parked next to the drainage ditch by the side of the road and walked over there. The woman was Bernina Tobin, head of the Friends of the Perdido. When she saw him, she slammed the car's trunk and hurried inside the house.

Timothy went around to the makeshift building at the rear of the lot and knocked on its door. No response. An old van with a license plate holder from a Sacramento dealership stood at an odd angle to the structure, as if its driver had been in too much of a hurry to park it properly. Openshaw had probably gone somewhere on foot.

Another advantage to a town like this: if you knew enough about a person, you could figure out what establishments he would frequent. Joseph would eat at the Blue Moon and do his drinking at the Deluxe. It was not yet dinnertime, and the Deluxe was only three blocks away. Timothy set out for it.

The bar was reasonably crowded, dark, and smoky. Its owner had probably never heard of the county's antismoking ordinances, Timothy thought, and they weren't enforced with any regularity, anyway. Many of the sheriff's deputies entrusted with that task could be found lighting up in here when their shifts ended.

He peered around and found Joseph Openshaw seated at a table with a long-limbed young woman whose dark hair swirled windblown about the collar of her blue sweater. The two were leaning across the table, conversing intensely. As Timothy crossed the room toward them, he ignored the hostile stares that many of the patrons aimed his way.

Openshaw looked up at his approach, dark eyes registering surprise. "Mr. McNear," he said.

"Mr. Openshaw." He directed his gaze at the woman. "And this is . . . ?"

"Jessie Domingo," the woman said. "Of Environmental Consultants Clearinghouse."

"Ah, yes. One of the people who came from New York to help the Friends." He looked around, located an empty chair. "May I join you two?"

"Why would you want to do that?" Openshaw asked.

Jessie Domingo put a hand on Joseph's arm, said to Timothy, "Please do."

He moved the chair to the table and sat, suddenly weary. It had been a long day, and he sensed there was a lot more to be gotten through.

"A drink?" the Domingo girl asked.

"Please. Scotch."

She looked at Openshaw. "Joseph?"

He hesitated, then shrugged and went to get it.

Timothy turned his attention to the young woman. She was quite attractive in a natural way, her face devoid of makeup, even lipstick. He wondered if she affected such a look in New York, or if there she transformed herself into one of the sleek, impeccably dressed women he'd seen on his infrequent visits to the city, crowding the Manhattan sidewalks as they went about business or pleasure. She smiled at him, seemingly content to await Openshaw's return in silence.

Joseph came back with the drink, placed it in front of Timothy on a napkin bearing a caricature of the bar's owner. Timothy waited a moment before picking it up, not wanting to seem as badly in need of liquid courage as he actually was. When he sipped, the cheap blend burned raw in his throat.

The two were watching him, curiosity plain in their eyes. He set the glass down and asked, "How private a conversation can we hold here?"

Openshaw looked around, and Timothy's eyes followed his somewhat amused gaze. The crowd was an eclectic one, ranging from those who had recently achieved drinking age to those he could count as his seniors. Singles, couples, larger groups — all were intent on their drinks or their pool games, their own conversations or solitary thoughts. After the initial flurry of interest in Timothy, no one was paying him any attention.

Openshaw said, "About as private as if you were in church talking to your confessor. What do you want?"

"Are you aware that Stephanie Pace is missing?"

The two exchanged a swift glance. Openshaw said, "What do you know about that?"

"Only this." He related what Curtis Hope had told him.

When he had finished, Openshaw drummed his fingertips on the tabletop, studying him. The Domingo girl was frowning, obviously trying to fit the information into some private mental scheme. Finally Openshaw said, "How did you know Steph had made an appointment to see Curt?"

This was the point where he would have to proceed cautiously. "She did so at my request."

"Why?"

"Because I felt it was time we resolved what happened the night Mack Kudge was murdered."

Openshaw glanced at Jessie Domingo, shifted uneasily in his chair. She returned his look with a puzzled one.

Joseph said to her, "I'll explain later." And to Timothy, "Why now? At this particular time?"

Tell the truth and perhaps all the dominoes will fall. Lie, and further jeopardize Miss Stephanie's life and safety.

Decision time, old man. What's it going to be?

Topple the dominoes, if necessary. For Miss Stephanie. You owe her that much.

"Because," he said, "the waterbaggers are blackmailing me for the use of my land, and I intend to put a stop to it."

Jessie Domingo

As the two men spoke, events of a night only six years after she was born unfolded in front of Jessie.

". . . came back from making my speech in Sacramento, found the body . . ."

". . . knew you'd moved it. Nobody else would've . . ."

". . . took it to the mill . . ."

". . . covered up for all three of us . . ."

". . . no, for myself . . . couldn't have anyone find out about my mistake with Stephanie . . ."

". . . or maybe you were in the house all along, McNear, and killed him . . ."

". . . can prove I wasn't . . ."

". . . then who?"

"Doesn't matter now. What *does* is that the waterbaggers claim they have an eyewitness who saw me moving the body. That's what they're holding over my head."

"How do you know they're not bluffing?"

"They have exact details: how I put him in the tarp, loaded him into the wheelbarrrow, cleaned up the blood . . ."

"So who is this witness?"

"You ought to know, Joseph."

"Me? Why?"

"I believe Stephanie when she says she never told. Curtis denies it, too, and I'm convinced he's being honest with me."

"Wait a minute! You're accusing *me* of going to those people with ammunition that would destroy the Perdido?"

"Maybe you weren't thinking about the river. Maybe your desire to destroy me overshadowed those feelings."

"Why would I want to destroy *you?* You never even crossed my mind after I left the Cape."

"I very much doubt that. You loved Stephanie and you've never forgiven me for my mistake with her."

"I wouldn't call it a mistake."

". . . Never mind that. The fact remains that you're the only one who could have told those people about what I did that night. You must have witnessed the whole thing."

The whole thing, Jessie thought. Something about the way he says that . . .

Joseph's face contorted, and he flattened his hands on the table, about to rise. "No way! When Curt and I left, Mack's body was just lying there in your garden. We went to the beach at Cauldron Creek and met Steph. She can corroborate that."

Jessie grabbed his arm, restrained him, and said, "Mr. McNear, who was it from Aqueduct Systems that contacted you?"

He looked at her, eyes blank for an instant. In the heat of the argument he'd forgotten she was there. "Gregory Erickson."

"Did he tell you how he located this eyewitness?"

". . . No."

"But his knowing the details frightened you enough that you were willing to grant them a right-of-way across your land."

"Yes."

"Why?"

"I don't understand the question."

"Moving a dead body is a crime, but not all that serious. And a long time has passed — maybe even the statute of limitations. I would think the authorities would be lenient with you, in view of your standing in the community."

Joseph added, "What I still don't understand is why you've suddenly changed your mind and are admitting what you did, after first caving in to the waterbaggers' pressure tactics."

"I thought I made that clear. Stephanie Pace is missing. My community is being torn apart. I can't sit by and do nothing."

Joseph said, "Very commendable. I wish I believed your motives were that unselfish. But since you insist you want to do something, what do you propose?"

"First we will find Stephanie. Then I will go public with the details of that night. It won't be easy on you or the others, but since I don't intend to press charges on the burglary —"

The door to the bar opened, and Curtis Hope stood there. His hair was wind tangled, his face ruddy with the cold. He spotted them and rushed over to the table. Confusion muddied his features when he recognized McNear. "What're you doing here?" he asked him.

"Speaking of the same matters as I did with you."

"Busy, aren't you?" He hesitated. "Well, I found something. I don't know if it's got to do with Steph disappearing or not, but after we talked, I went to the beach at Cauldron Creek and looked around. This was lodged between the rocks where I found the blood." He held out an old-fashioned wrist-watch with a leather band that had torn loose on one side.

Joseph leaned forward. "I've never seen it before. McNear?"

McNear held out his hand, examined it for a long moment, then shook his head.

Curtis said, "Maybe the cops can trace it."

"And how long d'you think that would take?" Joseph asked. "We need to find Steph right away."

"How?"

"She has a lot of friends in this town; I say we contact them and mount a search tonight. In the meantime you" — he motioned at McNear — "go to the sheriff's department and get them started on an official investigation. Tell them everything, if you have to."

McNear nodded, his face gray and waxen.

"How can I help?" Jessie asked.

"You wouldn't be of much use in the search," Joseph said. "It's getting dark, and it'll be hard enough for people who know the territory. But there is one thing you can do: those reports on Erickson and Woodsman that Eldon received — contact that private investigator and find out what was in them. If the information is damaging to either, maybe Eldon planned to use pressure tactics on him."

She nodded. "I'll try, even if I have to go to San Francisco and meet with Tom Little in person."

"Okay," Joseph said. "Curt, you come with me, and we'll mobilize a search party."

As the two men left the bar, Jessie turned to speak to McNear, but again he seemed to have forgotten her presence. In his eyes was the greatest expression of sadness she'd ever seen, and his long, slender fingers moved over the face of the old watch as if it were a talisman.

Joseph Openshaw

The searchers assembled in the parking lot of the Blue Moon, bundled against the cold, flashlights in hand. Joseph had been able to rally most of the Friends; the restaurant staff had contacted other locals; Curtis had enlisted a number of people from the rez. Arletta and Tony had closed the restaurant and turned it into a headquarters where they would field calls and relay any news to the searchers via cell phones. As everyone spread out into the night, heading toward the areas they knew best, Joseph felt a faint stirring of hope.

By now Timothy McNear would have contacted the sheriff's department. By now a story suppressed for two decades had been aired. McNear had said he would not press charges against Steph, Curt, and Joseph for the burglary, but — in the absence of other viable suspects — they would come under suspicion of Mack Kudge's murder. Even if they were cleared, their friends and neighbors would never regard them in the same way.

Well, maybe that was the incentive all three of them needed to jump-start the lives that had been stalled all those years ago. Maybe it was the incentive he and Steph needed to jump-start the relationship that had been there all along in spite of his denials.

If they found Steph. If they found her alive . . .

Steph Pace

No light at all coming under the door now, and she was cold. Her head ached, and her mouth was dry and she was beginning to hear things.

Footsteps. They were there, and then they weren't.

Voices. Or perhaps it was only the wind in the trees.

I'm losing my mind.

Get a grip on yourself.

I can't hold it together much longer.

You've got to. If he comes back, you know what you have to do.

And you know who he is. He made a mistake with you, a bad one that you didn't even realize till now.

She hugged herself but didn't stop shivering. Tried to convince herself that knowing her enemy was half the battle, but that didn't help, either.

More footsteps that weren't footsteps.

More voices that were only wind rattling the palm fronds.

Another spasm of shivers hit her, worse

than any she'd experienced before. She hugged herself tighter, rocked back and forth in an effort to generate some body heat.

Hold it together. You can do it. Hold on!

Timothy McNear

Timothy laid the watch on his kitchen table, pulled the phone toward him, and punched in half of the number he knew by heart but had never called. Then he broke the connection and stared at the instrument as if it were a weapon he was about to turn upon himself.

I should have known. The look — it was there in his eyes on Saturday.

Denial, old man. Denial.

Again he started to dial, but this time only got as far as the international calling code. Couldn't finish, because once the call was completed and his questions asked, he'd be forced to confront the futility of the sacrifice he'd made. And then he'd have to do what he should have done all those years ago.

Maybe they'll find Miss Stephanie quickly. Maybe all this will go away.

In twenty years it hasn't gone away, no matter how much you wished it would. What makes you think it will now?

He lifted the receiver and dialed 011, and then 61, the calling code for Australia.

Jessie Domingo

The private investigator, Tom Little, was adamant: he wouldn't reveal the contents of the reports he'd messengered to Eldon Whitesides, on grounds of client confidentiality.

"I appreciate your concern, Mr. Little," she said, "but Mr. Whitesides's life may be at stake. As well as a woman's."

"Perhaps if the request were coming from a law enforcement agency, I might consider releasing copies to them —"

"I can give you the name of the investigating officer here —"

"But I'd still need a court order."

"Mr. Little, I don't think you understand the gravity of the situation —"

"And I don't think you understand my obligation to my client. You may work for ECC, but this particular investigation was conducted for Mr. Whitesides, personally."

"I realize that. And since your client is in danger —"

"I'm sorry to hear that, but I could open up myself to a lawsuit, put my license at risk."

"I doubt Mr. Whitesides would sue you for helping us find him."

"How do I know what you're telling me is the truth?"

"You can verify the situation with the Soledad County Sheriff's Department. If you call and, as a good citizen, offer the reports —"

"I would still be putting myself at risk. My professional ethics would be compromised."

Jessie closed her eyes, thought quickly. "How about this: I'll tell you what I think was in those reports, and you confirm or deny it."

". . . What do you think was in them?"

"That one of the men under investigation has a personal link to Soledad County. A personal link to Timothy McNear, the man you investigated for Environmental Consultants Clearinghouse."

"I don't think I should answer that."

"Please, Mr. Little. I'm begging you."

A long pause.

"Mr. Little?"

". . . All right. You would be correct in assuming that."

"Which man — Gregory Erickson or Neil Woodsman?"

"I've said more than I should have, Ms. Domingo. And that is all I have to say."

Joseph Openshaw

Joseph fought the wind as he walked north from the ancient landslide at Cauldron Creek Beach to the sea caves that undermined the cliffs. His shoes and jean legs were soaked from the waves that had pounded the rock formations as he'd scrambled over them. Windblown sand scoured his face, forcing him to squint.

The cave's mouth was triangular, narrow. He squeezed his upper body through it, raising his flashlight. Nothing but striated walls, a sandy floor, and water steadily dripping from somewhere overhead. He eased out again and continued up the beach.

The other cave was much larger, with an arched opening. He ducked his head as he entered, straightened, and shone the light around. On the ground lay a foul-smelling heap of kelp that had washed in on the high tide; the thick coils were intertwined like a nest of garter snakes. He stepped over them, moved toward the back of the cave, where it branched off into two chambers. The first of these was nearly filled in by a slide, but in the other were the remnants of a campfire.

He wriggled through the opening, knelt down to feel the ashes.

Cold and damp. Crushed beer cans lay nearby, the colors of their labels fading. Long time since anyone had been there.

Long time since Joseph had been there, too. Not since the night of Mack's murder. He and Curt had driven from McNear's to the beach in silence; Steph had arrived fifteen minutes later with the money. They'd buried it under a cairn of rocks, and as far as he knew, it was still there.

We'll come back for it someday.

We'll never come back. Mack died for that money.

All right, then we'll leave it buried.

And we won't talk about tonight again. Okay?

How can we not talk about it?

Leave it buried like the money. Leave it.

Joseph raised his flashlight and shined it around. The cairn was still there, apparently undisturbed. After this was over, he'd dig up the money and return it to McNear. The first of several atonements he'd make.

Steph Pace

She'd stopped listening to the footsteps and the voices. They were all products of her imagination. Stopped shivering, too; she was beyond cold now. Thirst? Hunger? Beyond them, too. Pain? Numbness was more like it.

Her increasing lack of sensation brought with it a strange clarity of mind. Her thoughts had never been more reasoned. Calm, too. Accepting.

She was going to die.

Here, alone, in this cold, silent prison. Here, or somewhere else, at the hands of the man who had taken her. Didn't matter which. Or how.

What it all came down to was that she was going to die.

And she simply didn't care.

Timothy McNear

Timothy went to the den and unlocked the lower right-hand drawer, removed the .38 revolver and the box of bullets. Then he sat down and began loading the weapon.

It was well preserved, in perfect working order. It had rested there in the drawer since the night it was used to kill Mack Kudge. He hadn't been able to bring himself to do the intelligent thing and get rid of it — toss it into the sea off the pier at the mill, or lose it in one of the deep canyons of the coastal ridge.

Perhaps he'd unconsciously been keeping it for this occasion. Perhaps on some level he'd always known that the time would come when he'd need it.

The gun loaded, he raised it and sighted along its barrel. He'd been a good shot, as most country boys were, and he had no doubt he still was. At least good enough for what he might do tonight, if necessary.

He stood, thrust the revolver into the

side pocket of his parka. Then he went back to the kitchen for the old watch that had once belonged to his father.

Time to go.

Jessie Domingo

Damn Tom Little and his client confidentiality! Professional ethics, my ass! He's just trying to cover his.

Jessie snatched up the phone receiver and called the sheriff's department substation in Calvert's Landing. The clerk put her through immediately to Rhoda Swift.

"That investigator Eldon Whitesides had working for him . . ." she began.

"Tom Little, yes." Swift sounded distracted.

"Have you spoken with him?"

"I have a call in, but he hasn't returned it."

"Well, I just reached him on his cellular. He won't give out much information, but apparently there's some personal connection between either Gregory Erickson or Neil Woodsman and Timothy McNear."

"Well, of course. McNear has given them permission to —"

"No, not a business connection. Personal."

"I see." Now she had Swift's interest.

"Is Mr. McNear still there?" Jessie asked.

"Here, at the substation?"

"Yes. He should've come in by now."

"Why?"

"He . . . You haven't seen him?"

"I haven't seen Mr. McNear since we met a couple of days ago with Mr. Erickson, to discuss the investigation into the destruction of the water bag."

My God, maybe McNear never really intended to go to the authorities. But he seemed sincere. Maybe he's just a slow driver. Maybe . . . Well, no use speculating on that now.

"Ms. Domingo," Swift said, "can you tell me what this is all about?"

"I'll let Mr. McNear do that when he gets there. But I think you'll want to talk with Tom Little. His report was delivered by courier to Eldon Whitesides shortly before he disappeared." Quickly she read off the investigator's cellular number and then broke the connection.

Maybe Swift's official status would persuade Little to give up his files, but Jessie doubted it; he'd probably insist on a court order. It was, it seemed, up to her to make sense of the situation. She reached for her laptop.

During one of her disastrous bad-boy romances with an investigative reporter, she'd helped him with a research project, and while she'd come away from the relationship with the usual emotional scars, she'd also acquired some invaluable skills. Now she waited for the slow dial-up Internet service to connect, and when it did, she accessed a site called Who?.com and tapped in Gregory Erickson's name.

Joseph Openshaw

When Joseph pulled into the parking lot at the Blue Moon, there were only a few cars in the slots. He got out of the van and hurried inside, found Tony behind the bar, talking with Arletta.

"Any word?" he asked.

"Nothing yet. Curt got a search organized up on the rez and came down here looking for you. He's in the kitchen."

Joseph went back there, found Curt drinking orange juice directly from a large container. When he saw Joseph, he offered it to him and said, "Keeps your strength up."

Joseph took it, had a drink, passed it back. "What's up?"

"I decided the folks at the rez can carry on without me. Thought you and I might take a ride down to the mill. Lots of places there where you could hide a person, or a —"

"Or a body," Joseph finished for him.

"Look, man, you can't think like that."

"You are."

"That's just me. I kind of got into a

negative way of thinking a long time ago. Turned it around when I started studying the old ways, but sometimes I backslide."

Joseph thought of the shrine he'd seen in Curt's bedroom; so the spiritual beliefs of their people were what occupied his old friend these days.

"You really believe in all that?" he asked.

Curt shrugged. "Man's gotta believe in something. Let's you and I concentrate on believing Steph's gonna come back to us okay. So do we check the mill?"

"We check the mill."

Steph Pace

The footsteps and the voices melded together and soothed her like a lullaby. She curled into a ball on the floor, arms wrapped around her knees. Her pulse beat slowly in counterpoint. Her eyes closed, and she drifted. . . .

". . . This is insane!"

"So was you killing Eldon Whitesides."

"That was entirely different. He was trying to use what the detective found out to force us out of here. We were struggling for the report; I pushed him. It was an accident. But this is cold-blooded murder . . ."

"No way you can prove your story without my corroboration."

"Right. You've already made that clear. But I don't see why it's necessary to kill her."

"I told you, I made a slip. Called her 'Miss Stephanie,' and she recognized me — I could see it in her eyes. She could've ruined everything for us."

". . . Well, all right, let's get it over with."

Steph jerked her head up, looked wildly

around. Those were real voices. Real footsteps.

And she recognized both speakers.

"How'd you get the key to this place, anyway?" Gregory Erickson asked.

A low laugh. "It was where it's always been — on top of the door frame. Some things never change."

Some people never change, either. They just become more themselves. Greed, selfishness, cruelty — they go on and on.

A key scraped against a lock on the other side of the door.

Act like you're unconscious.

Steph lowered her head again, held her breath, waited. The door opened, and the men stepped in. A foot nudged her shoulder. She forced herself not to flinch, lying limp.

Clammy fingers grasped her wrist and felt for a pulse. "She's alive, probably comatose," Neil Woodsman said. "Won't take much to finish her off once we get her there."

"Christ, Neil!"

"You do what you have to. Whitesides and his detective's report are gone. She's the only one besides the old man who can make a connection. And even if he does, he'll never talk."

"I'm still nervous about that detective."

"You think he wants any part of this, mate? I know that kind of guy. The law comes around asking him questions about Whitesides, and he'll bury that report deep."

Hands grasped Steph's shoulders and pulled her into a sitting position. An arm slipped under her knees. Neil Woodsman was strong; he smelled of an unpleasant aftershave lotion. She willed herself to remain still as he lifted her and carted her from the potting shed, scraping her head on the door frame. The night was cold and breezy; palm fronds rustled overhead.

Woodsman shifted her, grunted, and said, "Give me a hand, will you?" Erickson grasped her feet, and they slung her between them. Together they hauled her through the garden, over the stone wall, then downhill.

A small hope was born in her. Wherever they were taking her, she might find a chance to escape. As long as they thought she was unconscious.

The men stopped abruptly, and then Erickson set her feet on the ground. Woodsman kept a tight grip on her shoulders. There was a sound that she identified as a trunk lid opening. Erickson grabbed her feet again.

The men lifted her and placed her on her side in the trunk, bending her legs at the knees. The lid slammed above her. She shuddered, forcing down a moan.

In moments the car started up and began moving.

Timothy McNear

The gun weighed heavy in his pocket. He shifted it some, keeping one hand firmly on the wheel. The headlights of an oncoming car blinded him, and he focused on the shoulder until it passed. Then darkness rushed at him as he started up the series of switchbacks.

He'd always appreciated irony, and he took grim pleasure in his choice of weapon. He actually felt himself smiling, but when he glanced in the rearview mirror, what he saw resembled a corpse's rictus.

Well, that was appropriate, wasn't it?

Eyes front, old man. This is no time to drive off the cliff. You've got a job to do.

A job you should have done long ago.

Jessie Domingo

Frowning, Jessie hit the "Back" icon and once more typed in the name "Neil Woodsman." She clicked on "Search" and waited.

Again she came up with no match.

The man didn't exist. How could that be?

She reached into her briefcase for her information on Aqueduct Systems and found the profile of Woodsman. Administrative assistant to Gregory Erickson since January of last year. Formerly with Resources Management, Ltd., of Melbourne, Australia. The same firm where Erickson worked before establishing Aqueduct Systems.

She turned back to the laptop and ran a search for Resources Management. No mention of Woodsman's name in connection with it. Another damn dead end. Or was it?

Australia . . .

His accent was Australian, not British. And he'd lied about having most recently lived in the UK.

Australia . . .

Fitch had left most of his paper files with her when he went to Sacramento. She sifted through them for the private investigator's report on Timothy McNear and read it slowly. And then began another search.

Joseph Openshaw

"Jesus Christ, this place is big," Curt said. "We should've brought reinforcements."

"Yeah, we should've."

Joseph stepped over a fallen timber and promptly lodged his foot between two others. He eased it out. The air at the burned-out mill site was cold, thick with the after-smell of smoke and fire-retardant chemicals. The wind blew strongly off the sea, making a loose piece of piping on one of the collapsed buildings clang monotonously. A car's engine growled in the distance, and a semi geared down on the switchback.

They'd been searching for half an hour, beginning at the northern boundary of the property. Most of the wooden buildings had burned to the ground or collapsed, but there were a number of corrugated iron sheds still standing that must be searched thoroughly. There was enough moonlight that they didn't need their flashlights to move about the ground, but each time they entered one of the sheds, they turned them on and shone their beams around. Each time they found a structure empty, Joseph didn't know whether to be relieved or disappointed.

A burned-out skeleton loomed in front of them. "What's that over there?" he asked Curt.

"Part of the old admin building. Enough of it's standing to hide somebody in."

"Let's go, then."

Curt didn't move. "I'm thinking maybe we ought to give it up for now. Just till morning, when we can see."

"No. I'm not giving up, not when there's a chance we can find her tonight."

"You really love her, don't you, man?"

"Yeah. I guess I never stopped."

"Well, then, we'll find her, bring her home — What's that?"

"Where?"

"Over there. Somebody moving."

Joseph turned to peer across the moonlit landscape. "You're imagining things."

"No, I'm not. Look out there, on the pier."

Now Joseph saw them — two shadowy figures with something slung between them, moving slowly, bent over by its weight.

Steph?

Simultaneously the two of them began to run.

Steph Pace

She must have passed out at some point, because all at once she was aware of cold air and hands grasping her limbs again. She was no longer in the car's trunk, but being carried somewhere. All around her was the smell of damp, burned wood and the sea.

The mill. They'd taken her to the mill.

"For God's sake, mate, don't drop her," Woodsman said.

"I still don't like this."

"You don't have to like it. I said before, you do what you have to. And you, in particular, have to. Unless you want the fact that you killed Whitesides to come out."

"You're threatening me?"

"I'm telling you, it's too late to turn back now."

Steph opened her eyes. The men were staggering along the pier. She could hear the partially deflated water bag sloshing in the dark water alongside it.

Going where? A boat?

"Dammit!" Woodsman stumbled, righted himself.

In a labored voice, Erickson asked, "When're the waste management people coming?"

"Barge'll be here at eight a.m. sharp."

Barge? She'd heard that the water bag was to be towed out to sea and scuttled. . . .

Oh, no, they're not going to do that to me!

Steph began to struggle. The men stopped as she flopped sideways, kicked out with her right foot.

"She's conscious!" Erickson exclaimed, nearly losing his grip.

She kicked harder but couldn't break free.

"Help me swing her over the rail!"

"We can't —"

"Just do it!"

She twisted and wriggled furiously. It did no good. As one, they swung her up and over, her back scraping the railing. She cried out as they let go of her, and then she was plummeting down, smacking hard into the water.

Cold — oh, Jesus Christ, cold!

Her head went under, and she began to sink.

Can't breathe. Can't swim.

She tried to kick, but her legs felt leaden. Water poured up into her nose and down her throat, making her choke and gasp. Then, suddenly, her feet hit bottom; she pushed off, clawing upward through the icy water. Her head bumped against something, and she struck out wildly. Her hands touched the rubberized bag.

She shoved frantically at the bag. It was heavy, unyielding. With flagging strength she scissor-kicked to one side.

And then her head broke the surface. She gasped, spitting water, feeling the cold air's bite in her throat and lungs.

After a moment her panic receded, and she opened her eyes. She was in an air pocket inside the crumpled bag. Through a tear some six feet away, she could see the moonlit sky.

Got to get out of here.

She started to paddle toward the opening. Something bulky bobbed and nudged at her shoulder. She pushed it away. It nudged again, and she turned her head and looked . . .

Into the dead, staring eyes and bloated face of Eldon Whitesides.

Timothy McNear

Timothy parked his car in front of the motel office, went inside, and asked for Neil Woodsman's room number. The clerk, a heavyset woman whom he'd seen around town, said, "Number eleven," and pointed at the far wing.

Timothy thanked her and hurried out. For a moment he stood next to his car, breathing the crisp air. The night was star-shot, beautiful, with a brisk offshore breeze. A perfect evening in a horribly imperfect world.

He put his hand on his pocket, felt the reassuring weight of the revolver. He'd never liked hunting, had only done it to please his father. He liked it even less now, but it was a necessity.

A logging truck barreled past, going too fast for what the sign at the edge of town referred to as a "congested area." Timothy watched its taillights flash as it swung into the switchback; then he turned and walked toward room eleven. Faint light shone around the window curtains. He paused briefly before he knocked.

No response. He knocked again.

Empty, despite the light.

As he started to turn away from the door, a woman's voice said behind him, "I've already checked, Mr. McNear. Your grandson isn't here."

Jessie Domingo

McNear turned toward her, his face slack with shock. After a moment he said, "How did you find out?"

"I ran an Internet search. Neil Woodsman doesn't exist, but Shelby McNear worked for the same Australian company as Gregory Erickson. I guess when he heard Erickson was interested in harvesting water from the Perdido, he went to him and exchanged his leverage over you for a job."

"Yes. Shelby is our mysterious eyewitness."

"Why didn't you recognize him, your own grandson?"

"I only saw him at a distance until we were both on the podium the day the waterbag was shot. The beard, the accent. And he was only twelve when his father took him to Australia."

"What made you realize?"

"The watch Curtis Hope found on the beach. It was my father's, and I passed it on to Shelby before they left." He paused, shaking his head. "I've been incredibly stupid. The witness couldn't've been anyone but Shelby. He was there in the house that night twenty years ago — he'd gotten sick, so his father left him behind with me when he and Max went to San Francisco two nights before their sailing. I was committed to a speaking engagement in Sacramento the night before I was to bring him down to the ship, and I thought he was old enough to be left alone. I couldn't have been more wrong."

McNear paused, shaking his head. If possible, he looked sadder than he had earlier at the Deluxe. "Tonight I talked with my son in Australia — the first time in all these years — and he said Shelby was working in North Carolina. That confirmed it."

"Your son — why were you estranged?" Jessie asked.

"Because of a mistake I made long ago with a young girl."

"What kind of mistake?"

". . . Actually, it wasn't a mistake at all. A criminal act. Attempted rape. Robert found out, and he already knew I'd been unfaithful to his mother. It was the last straw; he didn't want his boys exposed to a person like me, so he moved halfway around the world."

This old gentleman, a rapist? It hardly seemed possible. But, then, molesters came in all guises. . . .

"Don't judge me," McNear added. "I've already judged myself."

After a moment she said, "It's not my business to judge you. You're the one who has to live with it. You and the poor girl, whoever she was. Did your son turn your grandsons against you?"

"Yes. The one time I wrote them, I received a return letter full of hate from Shelby."

"Let me ask you this: do you know who killed Mack Kudge?"

McNear looked away.

"You do know. Was it you?"

"No, I only disposed of his body."

Now she understood his anguish. "We'd better find your grandson."

"Yes."

"And we shouldn't go alone. Let's see if we can find Joseph or Curtis."

Joseph Openshaw

Before he and Curtis could reach the pier, the two men dropped their burden over the railing. The loud splash that followed brought an involuntary cry from Joseph's throat, sent him into a headlong rush.

Now he recognized Gregory Erickson and Neil Woodsman. And as soon as they saw him coming, they broke and fled, angling in the opposite direction across the pier.

Curt yelled, "Cut them off!" and ran a flanking maneuver.

The men kept running. Woodsman wasn't looking where he was going, and he banged into the rail and staggered. Erickson swung his head from side to side in a panic, then veered off in another direction.

Joseph measured the distance between himself and Woodsman, went up on the balls of his feet and launched his body through the air. His shoulder and grasping hands caught Woodsman at the knees and brought him down. Woodsman cried out as he hit the ground, then began to struggle. Joseph clung to him, looking up in time to see Erickson scrambling toward the ruins of the mill.

"Let him go!" Joseph called to Curt. "Help me with this one!" Woodsman twisted, smacked Joseph in the head with his fist. The blow made him bite his tongue; then another smashing blow sent pain down his arm and into his fingers. He lost his grip on Woodsman, and the man began to scramble away. Joseph pushed up, staggered forward, got his arms tight around Woodsman's waist and brought him down again. Then Curt was there, catching hold of the bastard's arms and pinning him facedown.

Joseph stood, wiping blood from his lip, grabbed Woodsman's head by the hair and shook it. "What did you drop over the side? Was it Steph?"

Woodsman made unintelligible sounds.

"Damn you, was it Steph?"

". . . Yes . . ."

"Jesus!" He let go of Woodsman's hair, and ran down the pier, holding his shoulder, calling out to Steph. He leaned over the rail and peered frantically down at the water bag, yelled her name.

No answer, and no motion other than the natural sloshing of the water.

Steph Pace

Shuddering violently, she pushed Whitesides's body away. The motion of the waves returned it. She gave it a harder shove, fighting off nausea, and began dog-paddling as fast as she could toward the opening in the bag.

From above, she heard the sounds of running feet and shouting — a voice bellowing her name.

Joseph!

Her lungs were burning, and blood roared loud in her ears. Her limbs were starting to go numb. She couldn't respond, just kept paddling. Whitesides's corpse nudged at her feet.

"Steph! Steph!"

Close to the opening . . .

The weight of the water was dragging her down.

So close . . .

Her breath came shorter.

And then she was there. She reached up with leaden arms, tore at the bag's ragged edges.

"Steph! Oh, my God . . ."

Joseph's contorted face looked over the rail at her, and then he vaulted it and plunged into the water. He folded his long arms around her, pulled her close. He was warm, so warm. She pressed her face against the rough fabric of his parka as he yelled for help.

Safe. Safe at last.

Timothy McNear

The Domingo girl drove Timothy's car through the gates of the mill. "Look!" she said. "Lights, over by the pier."

Stationary headlight beams burned at the front of an old van. The one he'd seen earlier, parked at Joseph Openshaw's place.

The girl accelerated, and the car bumped over the rise and coasted down the other side, weaving among scattered debris. She slammed on the brakes and jumped out without shutting off the motor. Timothy followed.

The side door of the van was open, and Stephanie Pace sat inside, wrapped in a gray blanket. Joseph Openshaw was leaning in to speak with her. Some distance away he saw Curtis Hope standing at the foot of the pier, arms folded across his chest as he guarded a figure that lay on the concrete.

Timothy's breath caught. He heard the girl make a startled exclamation, but he ignored her and kept going, eyes on the prone body trussed up with a heavy length of rope. The bound man turned his head at Timothy's approach. Neil Woodsman.

No, not Woodsman. His grandson Shelby. The look was there in his eyes: anger and, even in this situation, arrogance. At times he'd been a hateful, greedy little boy, and he had grown into a hateful, greedy man.

This is what I risked everything for.

Now Timothy felt his long-repressed anger surface. He stared at Shelby, and damned if the young bastard didn't curl his lip in contempt.

Timothy's hand moved to his pocket, his fingers caressing the gun. He brought it out and leveled it at Shelby's head.

"What . . . ?" Curtis Hope said.

"Mr. McNear!" the Domingo girl called.

He paid no attention to them.

The arrogance and contempt faded from Shelby's face. Then something akin to a fog bank passed over it. His eyes showed fear. His lip quivered, and he strained at the rope, whimpering.

Curtis Hope stepped forward.

"Keep away," Timothy told him.

The Domingo girl came closer. "Mr. McNear . . ."

"Stay back," he ordered.

"Grandfather," Shelby said, a sob

catching in his throat. "Please!"

Timothy studied him dispassionately. Shelby's tone and expression now resembled those of the twelve-year-old boy who had admitted to shooting Mack Kudge and begged for his help.

A noise downstairs woke me up. I took the gun and went to look. There was a man on the patio. I only wanted to scare him; I didn't know the gun was loaded. But then he came at me, and I pulled the trigger. Help me. Please!

But Shelby had seen Timothy load the gun only days before. And Mack Kudge had been shot in the back.

Shelby had been acting then, and he was acting now.

"Please, Grandfather!"

Two decades, and nothing's changed, except for the worse.

Timothy held the gun on Shelby a moment longer, then slowly lowered it. He couldn't do it. It wasn't in him to kill anyone, for any reason.

"I've sacrificed enough for you," he said. "The law can have you now."

Shelby closed his eyes.

Timothy turned and walked away.

Thursday, February 26

Jessie Domingo

Jessie hugged Steph, then Joseph. Made the usual promises about keeping in touch: if you're ever in New York . . . maybe I'll get out here for a vacation . . . would really be nice to see you again . . . Then she turned, took the pilot's hand, and stepped up into the small plane. Fitch, who had returned from Sacramento the previous morning, was already there, and he helped her find the ends of her seat belt.

"Am I ever glad to be going home!" she said.

"Me, too."

"Even if I'm probably out of a job."

"I don't think you have anything to worry about. The foundation's board will appoint an interim director until they can hire someone permanent, and ECC's work'll go forward as usual."

"Will it? I wonder. Eldon, for all his faults, was heart and soul of the operation. Besides, I'm not sure I want to stay on there."

His preflight checks made, the pilot

started the engine and began taxiing. Jessie turned to the window to wave to Joseph and Steph, but they were already walking back to his van.

Fitch said, "Well, what else would you do?"

"I don't know. My immediate plans are to sleep for a week, now that we don't have to worry about waterbaggers."

"Temporarily, you mean. An Alaskan water-harvesting firm is snooping around up in Humboldt County. This is an issue that's not going to go away until it's resolved by the courts."

"Well, you're the man to do that."

Fitch smiled. "Jess, I've been thinking . . ."

"Yes?"

"I've learned a lot from you during our time out here. We make a good team. I've expanded my practice; I could use a good researcher and client contact person."

The offer surprised her. Pleased her, too. "I might consider that."

"Client contact is an area where I really need help. As you once pointed out, my personality —"

"Could use some work. But nobody's perfect."

And nobody needs to be perfect. That's what I've learned out here. Even Casey isn't perfect

— *I just don't see her flaws. I'm going to start being* me *now, rather than trying to be somebody else.*

Fitch said, "I'm glad to hear you say so."

"What?"

"That nobody's perfect. Anyway, we'll have the whole flight to New York to compare our flaws and make some plans."

"Yeah — with you in business class and me in coach."

"Oh, I meant to tell you: I had some extra frequent flyer miles, so I upgraded your ticket. Only the best for my prospective employee."

Joseph Openshaw

"Coffee," Joseph said to Steph. "No, a beer. To celebrate the demise of the waterbaggers."

She went behind the bar, got two IPAs, and returned to the booth where he was sitting. "Don't say 'demise.' I've been having nightmares about Eldon Whitesides's corpse."

He shook his head. "Not a pretty image. Jesus, what a place to dispose of a body."

"Gives a whole new meaning to burial at sea. But I don't want to talk about that, not till they bring Erickson and Woodsman — McNear, I mean — to trial."

"Deal." Joseph toasted her.

Steph stared moodily around the bar area. Her eyes were deeply shadowed, her face gaunt. It would take a while for her to mend, and Joseph wanted to be part of her healing process.

"What're you thinking about?" he asked.

"Another month of winter vegetables."

"Profound."

"Very." She hesitated. "Actually, I was

thinking how sick I am of the Blue Moon. And Cape Perdido. And Soledad County."

"Remember how we used to talk about leaving?"

"I do."

"Denver, Chicago, New York — Europe, even. We could still do that."

"We could."

"No reason I couldn't continue with my pro-environmental work in another place, or another country. But my first order of business is in Sacramento."

"Oh? What's that?"

"To find out who embezzled that hundred and fifty thousand from the Coalition. Clear my name, so to speak. Now that I've returned McNear's three thousand to him, I feel the need to set the rest right."

Steph's eyes narrowed, and her mouth pulled down.

"What?" he asked.

"Don't you think there's another order of business that's more important?"

Now, where was this sudden anger coming from? He raised his eyebrows questioningly.

"Don't you think it's time you set it right with us?"

"Things *are* right. Aren't they?"

"No. You walked out on me years ago. Then you came back and acted as if we'd never been anything to each other. Just because we've been through an ordeal together doesn't mean you can suddenly assume that everything's the way it used to be."

She was right, of course. After a moment he asked, "So what d'you want me to do?"

"Take it slowly. Let us get to know each other again, before we contemplate running off together. You owe me that."

"Yeah, I do." His eyes locked on hers, and he covered her hand with his. She didn't pull away. "Us — it's not impossible, is it? That we could get it back together?"

"No, it's not impossible."

"Then it's possible."

"I suppose."

"*Very* possible," he said, and twined his fingers through hers.

Steph Pace

Steph decided to take the rest of the day off from the restaurant and try to get some sleep, but when she got home, she was afraid to lie down and close her eyes. The nightmares in which she was again trapped in the water bag with Eldon Whitesides's corpse had been persistent and terrifying. Finally she made a mental review of her to-do list and decided to clean her closet. Soon clothing was strewn all over her bed.

This shirt had never looked right on her. These pants were completely out of date. And, my God, this dress . . . Why on earth had she kept such things so long?

But then there was the colorful woven top from Africa. It would look great on a warm beach somewhere. And this long dress, tailored but romantic. She could picture wearing it in a hill town in Italy.

Italy. That was the place she and Joseph had talked about most in the old days.

Maybe they'd talk about it again in the days to come. Talking about anything seemed possible now that she'd started to express her anger with him. She had no doubt that she'd vent at him many times again — twenty years of smoldering resentment couldn't be expunged in one outburst — but at least she'd opened the channels of communication.

Maybe there was a future for them yet. . . .

Very possible.

She went to the living room, took down her atlas from the bookcase. Lugged it back to the bedroom, and pushed aside one of the piles of clothing. Then she curled up and opened it to the map of Italy.

She traced her finger over the map, spoke aloud names of places she'd only dreamed of: Roma, Firenze, Venezia, Napoli. Pictured vineyards, olive groves, villages that had changed little since ancient times. After a while she grew drowsy and pushed the book away, cradled her head in the crook of her elbow.

When sleep came, Steph's nightmare did not return.

Timothy McNear

Timothy stood at the foot of the pier. Yellow crime-scene tapes fluttered in the stiff offshore wind. Investigators and technicians had come and gone all day yesterday, but now the mill was deserted. He turned and began walking toward the ruins of the guard shack, where he'd left his car.

His grandson and Gregory Erickson — who had been apprehended at a Calvert's Landing motel, where he'd been holed up ever since he killed Eldon Whitesides — had been taken to the jail at Santa Carla and arraigned on attempted murder and murder charges respectively. Timothy had been questioned and released on his own recognizance; his lawyer was of the opinion that any potential charges would be dropped in exchange for his cooperation. Tomorrow his son Robert would arrive from Melbourne, and Timothy had agreed to meet his plane. He didn't have an inkling of how that reunion would go, was not even sure he cared. Recent events had taught him that one's past was best accepted and then left behind.

As he walked, he looked around at the devastation of his mill for the last time. Soon he would solicit bids on demolishing what was left and carting the wreckage away. And once that was done, he'd solicit more bids: for retrofitting the pier for sport fishing vessels, for landscaping, for a golf course and tennis courts. Over there, where the administration building had stood, would be the children's playground. And perhaps, in belated honor of Caroline, he'd plant a botanical garden. In the spring, when the egrets and great blue herons were nesting along the Perdido, work would begin.

And that, old man, will be your legacy.